STAR
BROTHER

STAR BROTHER

MAXINE ROSE SCHUR

Snowy Wings
PUBLISHING

TURNER, OREGON

We came into the world like brother and brother

And now let's go hand in hand, not one before the other.

—WILLIAM SHAKESPEARE

FIND THE THIRD STAR EAST OF SEGIN AND JUST SOUTH of Zorton. You will see that its light projects in a single beam across Earth's solar system, passing Mars, Venus, and the stars that spill like sugar across the sky. Find this star. Then with the certainty of science, line up the astronomical and geographical maps. Get out the compass, do the math. Plot the star's trajectory of light, so narrow and so precise, to where it falls to Earth in a pinpoint of starshine.

756 Keeler Street
North West Ithaca
New York

A large, lonely brick building. The southwest corner.

Light refracts when it contacts matter, of course. So, see that light bend right inside the third-floor dusty middle window, enter the building, and land—at last, with mystifying exactitude—on drawer #12428.

There it stops.

And there, in the drawer, neither dead nor alive and so long forgotten, waits a boy.

CHAPTER I

April 2, 2025

ON THAT FRIDAY AFTERNOON, THE GYM IN NEVADA'S Clearview High School buzzed with boredom. The Science Fair almost over, the morning's excitement had now been reduced to droning chit-chat. Teachers and parents milled about, while students stood guard over their projects. They were all dutifully waiting until four o'clock, when the judges would announce the winner, even though by three it was obvious who would win.

Well, that one of two would win. The rest should have just gone home.

Fair money was on Jessica Albright. Her project on the mutation of fruit flies had been written up by her father. Jessica's report had an expensive, published look, and when she explained her project, she spoke in such a poised manner, she easily hid the fact that she didn't know genes from beans.

Matthew Swundle was also a strong bet. He had been tutored by a zoology professor, for which his parents had paid good money. In the end, though, he'd just downloaded his report on the aggression of minks from the internet. Matthew's voice held all the excitement of roll-call, but he used such long words, even the judges couldn't tell he was all wrapper and no candy.

The three judges were just a trio of Clearview County's high school science teachers; yet that day, as they observed experiments and listened to memorized reports, they were like gods who held the choice, and thus the fate, of the one and only student-winner in their hands: the one who would win the ten-thousand-dollar Clearview City Science Scholarship. Jessica and Matthew were both prematurely gloating—until that extraordinary moment when everything changed.

It was the moment when the gym door banged open and Melanie Sandersborn, who had just presented on car ignition systems, gasped, "OH MY GOD!"

It was the moment the gym fell silent and all heads turned to see a thin, unkempt boy rush into the gym.

He carried no elaborate science project, simply a plastic folder which now broke open, spilling papers onto the gym floor.

"Jason!" Melanie cried. "He's *finally* shown up!"

Melanie raced toward him, helping him pick up his scattered papers, ignoring the other kids' snickers.

"Young man, you are late," said Mr. Kelman, the physics teacher and one of the judges.

"I had a little trouble with my project," Jason said as he stood up with a mess of papers in his hands.

"We have a little trouble with *you*," said another judge, the hated chemistry teacher, Mr. Malbrecht. "You are late. *Too* late. The fourth by-law of the Clearview County Science Competition states clearly that contestants are to give their reports by 3:30." Mr. Malbrecht fixed his eyes on Jason, while proclaiming loudly, "Rules are rules!"

"The fair ends in ten minutes," said the third judge, the biology teacher, Ms. Krulevitch. "Perhaps Jason may still have time to explain his project?"

Jason was a tall, thin sixteen-year-old with brown hair, pale skin, and sad green eyes. He had learned long ago to avoid looking at adults straight on, so he looked beyond them as he said, "Then the *judging* ends in ten minutes. I can explain my project in ten."

The judges glanced uneasily at each other.

"I think that might work, if you could . . ." Ms. Krulevitch began, but Mr. Malbrecht cut her off.

"WE CAN'T HAVE OUR SCIENCE FAIR DESCEND INTO CHAOS!" he bellowed. "RULES ARE RULES!"

"Excuse me," said Melanie Sandersborn as she came to stand before the judges, reading from a little spiral-bound book. "According to the Science Fair's sixth by-law, '*all contestants may have until four PM to explain and demonstrate their projects.*'" Then she added softly, "Rules are rules."

The judges looked at the earnest, dark-haired girl. Mr. Malbrecht frowned like a frog. But even he couldn't deny she had reminded them of the sixth by-law, so they had to let Jason speak.

Ms. Krulevitch turned to Jason and said, "Go."

Jason ran a hand through his hair as he began to explain his project. As he spoke, his usually quiet voice grew strong, and the indifference he wore as a protective cloak fell away.

"You know," Jason said, "every point in a hologram catches light waves that travel from every point in the object. So, looking at a hologram, you see exactly how light would have arrived at that point if you'd been looking *at the real object.* But if you just move your head around, the holographic image appears to change, just as the image of a real object changes—making it look three-dimensional. So, a cool thing about holograms is that, if you break a hologram into tiny pieces, you can still see the entire object in any of the pieces. I mean, like, if you smash a hologram of a glass vase into bits, you can still see the whole vase *in any of the bits!* Well, I figured, if this is true, then maybe I could create a kind of visual army by taking a photograph of someone, tearing it into bits, and turning it into a holographic image, then instantly reconstructing dozens, if not hundreds, or even thousands into that 3D holographic image."

Jason spoke with so much confidence and real interest, it was as if he had somehow transformed himself in the process, as if *he* were his own science project.

The judges, who had silently mocked Jason's binder

mess, now leaned toward the boy, intrigued. In fact, everyone in the gym was listening to him.

"I wanted to see if I could make my own little group of holograms as a kind of experiment," Jason continued. "It would prove my theory that you can get an exponential increase in the number of holographic images from a tiny fragment. Best of all, you could control the holograms from just your smartphone. I mean, right now, anyone can create 3D images from a smartphone, but they're not *real* holograms; they're videos of holograms and they appear only on the screen, without much color or movement. But the ones I've created are real and can be shown live, in real time, and best of all, they can appear outside the screen."

Jason looked up at the judges, and seeing they were listening to him, continued with greater confidence.

"The speed of light is 300,000 kilometers per second, but I found you can't always believe that. I mean, that's how fast light travels in outer space, but light can move slower than that too. So I created an app to slow light down, so my holograms look completely real. I worked it out mathematically."

He hurriedly put his jumbled papers in order, then

handed a copy of his theory to each of the judges.

But before they could read the first word, Mr. Malbrecht declared, "Not good enough! You haven't even put your last name on the paper! More important, simply talking or writing about something doesn't *prove* it." Mr. Malbrecht looked menacingly at Jason, then at the two other judges, who, though intrigued, were now intimidated by his pronouncement, so remained silent as Mr. Malbrecht went on. "Young man, a preposterous theory is not a proven theory. You have brought us messy papers, not a *science project.*"

"Oh, but I have," Jason replied.

He fished inside the right pocket of his jeans and pulled out an old smartphone. He scrolled and clicked on it until a photo of Mr. Malbrecht appeared on the screen. He held it high for all to see, as now, a crowd of kids, parents, and teachers had gathered about him. Jason swiped the screen again and again, so people could see he had numerous photos of Mr. Malbrecht on his phone. They showed Mr. Malbrecht in dozens of different attitudes and movements. Some pictures were just bits of Mr. Malbrecht—the scowl on his face, his caterpillar eyebrows, his over-polished shoes, his sausage-thick fingers, and his rear end as he bent over to tie his shoe. The gym erupted in guffaws and snickers, as obviously Jason had been secretly photographing the hated teacher for a good while. Yet this, in itself, was nothing extraordinary. But then, as the teachers looked on, conflicted between anxiety and curiosity—Jason made the impossible happen.

After he entered some code or something on the phone, each photo fragment reformed itself into a four-inch-tall, three-dimensional hologram of Mr. Malbrecht and popped right out of the phone! One after the other, they sprouted from the phone, dozens emerging, as if by magic. And they seemed to be alive! *So* real, *so* lifelike, were these holograms that, within moments, the gym seemed to be swarming with an army of mini Mr. Malbrechts.

The crowd in the gym erupted in screams and laughter.

Jason again entered something on his phone, and now the virtual army raced about like demented elves. Laughing maniacally, they scampered over the floor and, every now and then, one squeaked, "RULES ARE RULES!" as if rebuking the very air. A few ran up the wall and jumped down to the floor through the basketball hoop. One hopped inside a student's project about hamsters and ran inside the hamster wheel. Mr. Kelman tried in vain to seize one of the phantoms, as if it were a really small unruly pupil.

Mr. Malbrecht, pale and shaken, collapsed into a chair, overcome by the sight of himself—or rather *himselves*—running amok.

"Stop them!" he croaked.

But the screams and laughter in the gym drowned him out. Watching his mini selves getting stepped on and flattened out like cartoon characters—only to pop up again, good as new—made him feel weak. To add insult to injury, one of the creatures crawled up his back, sat on his shoulder like a pirate's parrot, and squawked, "RULES ARE RULES! RULES ARE RULES! RULES ARE RULES!"

The Clearview County Science Competition was now more like the Clearview County Carnival.

Jason poked at his smartphone, then *poof!*—the miniature Mr. Malbrechts disappeared. Everyone stood stunned, as if awakening from a weird dream, and the judges were shocked into silence, as if they'd witnessed the laws of the universe altered.

Mr. Malbrecht removed his glasses and wiped them, shakily and for too long. The two other judges alternately stared in wonder at Jason and read his theory. Despite the misbehavior of those micro-monsters, the boy had turned the established concept of holography as a photographic recording of a light field right on its head, destroyed long-held theories of optics, challenged the current method for 3D creation and, even more disquieting, posed a real threat to our assumptions about light, perception, consciousness, and yes—reality.

It was now four o'clock, yet the judges were stumped. Their job had always been to judge on the criteria of neatness, appealing quality of the project, organizational method, adherence to the competition rules, detailed oral explanation, and poise. Now they must judge a boy who spoke as a real scientist—a scrawny eleventh grader who not only had invented an astounding new technology but had also developed and proven *his own theory.*

A junior.

"Who helped you with this?" Mr. Malbrecht blurted

as he got back to his feet.

"No one," Jason answered.

"Come now," Mr. Kelman urged. "Certainly, you received *some* assistance from your parents?"

"I have no parents."

Ms. Krulevitch prodded gently, "Well, then some other relative, perhaps?"

"I have no relatives," Jason replied.

The judges had only minutes to decide the winner. When they returned exactly at 4:10, Ms. Krulevitch announced the name of Jason Atwood as the prizewinner of this year's Clearview County Science Competition, and then a lot of things happened:

1. The judges (even Mr. Malbrecht) shook Jason's hand on the makeshift award platform.

2. Mr. Kelman handed him a scholarship voucher for ten thousand dollars.

3. Jessica Albright burst into tears.

4. Matthew Swundle swore and threatened to juggle the judges like bean bags.

5. Matthew's parents shouted at each other about whose idiot idea it was to waste

money on a zoology professor.

6. Jason's math teacher, Ms. Marshall, beamed at him with a smile bright as a spotlight.

7. Melanie Sandersborn impulsively kissed Jason's cheek.

8. Jason put his cloak of indifference back on.

CHAPTER 2

"JASON, WILL YOU HELP ME GET MY PROJECT HOME?"

Jason, who was retrieving his books from his locker, turned to see Melanie. She was looking up at him with her blue eyes.

They're like little circles of sky, he thought. With her shiny black hair and pink-sunset cheeks, she was the prettiest girl he had ever seen.

"I dunno," he replied. No girl had ever asked him to walk her home before. He felt shyer than ever . . . awkward.

"Well, it's just that I could use some help. I mean . . . I live all the way at the far end of Laurel, and so do you."

"Oh yeah. Sure," Jason said. Why was he talking to his shoes? *Look her in the eyes*, he urged himself. But he didn't. He shut his locker door, set the lock, and followed her down the hall.

The gym was now almost empty, as most of the kids had already removed their science projects. Jason carefully stuck Melanie's heavy binder in his backpack, so she could carry the large batteries and other electrical parts in hers. Then, they stood in front of the enormous glass fish tank, lined on every side with mirrors, in which Melanie had placed her project, a small automobile ignition system, so you could see it working from all sides at once. He was glad he could focus on that.

"We need to hold the tank tightly from the bottom," Jason cautioned.

The two lifted the glass box and made their way slowly out of the gym. They walked up Hearne Street. Clearview was a small town that boasted mid-nineteenth-century buildings of Nevada's gold mining era. Now, the late afternoon sun bathed Clearview in a golden light so that, in those moments, Hearne Street looked more like a stage set than a real street. With their fragile burden, they walked very slowly, and Melanie chattered the whole way.

"I mean, you really were awesome! Did you see

Jessica's face? I thought she'd have a heart attack! And that jerk, Matthew! He was so mad! Oh, Jason, it's so exciting that you won! And just think, now you can go on to the Nevada competition!"

Jason couldn't see Melanie as she spoke, because the huge glass tank was between them and they had to keep their eyes on it as they walked. But in the bottom mirror, he could see her face reflected, smiling at him. She *was* pretty!

"It's on June fourteenth. What do you think?"

"I think the state competition is in the fall," Jason answered.

"Not the science competition. The dance—the *prom*!"

Jason saw Melanie's exasperated expression in the mirror and realized he hadn't been paying attention to what she was saying.

"What prom?"

"The Junior Prom, of course. Well . . . do you want to go? I think we'd have fun, and everyone will be going."

Jason felt his face turn red. He suddenly realized two things: Melanie Sandersborn had just invited him to the Junior Prom, and if he could see her reflection, she probably could see the reflection of his red face as well.

He had no money for the prom, though maybe he could get money from the Petersons. No, how many times had Mrs. Peterson told him, "Special circumstances for extra money must be kept to a minimum." But even if he had the money, did he *want* to go? What would be the point? Proms were for normal kids. Kids who had a mom and a dad and could hit them up for stuff like borrowing the family car. Kids who went on vacation. Kids whose last name came from their family, not from some social worker's imagination. Kids who didn't need to hoard food and could eat as much as they wanted. Kids who got hugged for no reason. Kids who weren't him. Besides, he couldn't dance, and then, well . . . Melanie was probably just being nice to him, simply because she was so nice. No, he had no business going to a prom with Melanie.

"I dunno," he said, keenly embarrassed and wishing he could just say yes.

He saw the hurt look in her eyes as she said quietly, "I just thought it might be fun. I . . ."

He never heard the rest of her sentence, for in the next moment, Jason was pushed hard from behind and flew onto the pavement. He landed against the streetlamp. Glass shattered with a sound like a whole street of doorbells ringing.

As Jason lay on the sidewalk, he heard Matthew yell, "JUNKYARD JASON!"

"MATTHEW!" Melanie screamed. "YOU JERK! YOU STUPID JERK!"

The rage that lived inside Jason rose to the surface. He wanted to hit Matthew as hard as any human could hit another. But Matthew had already run off.

A searing pain shot through Jason's leg. His pant leg was bloody. He rolled it up and found a long but superficial gash. On the sidewalk, Melanie's tank was now a clutter of broken glass, wires, and mirrors.

"Are you all right?" Melanie touched his arm.

"I'm OK."

He stood up, and in the process, smeared blood on his shirt.

"What's going on out here?" Mr. Darlington, owner of Darlington's Pharmacy, called to them from the doorway of his store. When he saw all the broken glass and Jason's bloody pant leg, he fetched a tube of antiseptic and bandages and inspected the cut on Jason's leg.

"No glass bits, that's good."

Mr. Darlington cleaned and bandaged Jason's cuts right there on the sidewalk, scolding all the while. "You kids are careless! Why in the world are you dragging all this junk around? Carrying glass is a recipe for disaster! Now, what's this? Another cut?" Mr. Darlington examined a small, hammer-shaped red mark on Jason's right forearm.

"That's nothing," Jason answered. "Just a birthmark."

"Good," Mr. Darlington answered. "One cut's enough. Now, you two wait here." He went back into his pharmacy.

Jason mumbled, "Sorry about your project."

There were tears in Melanie's eyes as she said, "Don't worry about it, Jason. I don't really need it anymore, anyway."

Mr. Darlington returned with a huge broom, a dustpan, and three big cardboard boxes. He handed Melanie and Jason thick rubber gloves. "Don't touch the glass without gloves, but clean it up well," he ordered. "I'll dump it in the bin in back of the pharmacy; I don't want folks slipping and cutting themselves."

Melanie and Jason cleaned up the glass in silence. Mr. Darlington took it away. Jason put his hands in his pockets, suddenly aware of their emptiness.

"Want to come to my house and have a snack?"

"I'd like to," he said, and at that moment, there was nothing more in the world he wanted to do but hang out with her. And yet, what would they do now, since what they had been doing was shattered and in a garbage bin at the back of the pharmacy? He found himself making something up. "But I'm sorry, Melanie, I can't. I've got to walk the Petersons' dog . . . right away."

"Oh, OK. See you tomorrow then." Melanie smiled at him, then turned and walked away.

He wanted to call out to her—tell her yes, he'd go to the prom with her, but he couldn't. Damn it! He *couldn't.*

CHAPTER 3

October 30, 1950
Ithaca, New York

*L*ILY *A*NNE *K*IMBLE *HAD JUST PLAYED THE CELLO AS IF* an angel had guided her. She was a concert cellist, and never missed the daily joy of drawing the bow across the strings to elicit what her husband, Herbert, called the "sounds of souls." Yet on this afternoon, in the quiet sunlight of her living room, she had felt inspired by the heavens.

Lily Anne let her hands once again stroke her belly. Soon, oh so soon, it would curve like the bottom of a lute, and when she thought of this image, she smiled. For though she had no idea whether this first baby would be a boy or a girl, she already loved it tenderly.

She put the cello and bow away in their case, then she went to the kitchen to prepare her afternoon tea.

When the tea was ready, she poured the amber liquid into the thin china cup, decorated with roses, and drank deeply. The tea made her think of her dear Herbert and what he would say if he saw her taking her afternoon tea.

"You cannot get England out of your veins," her husband teased.

But she didn't mind, for it was true. She often was homesick for England, and if a spot of tea eased that homesickness, well, she would keep what Herbert called her "curious custom."

She carried her cup over to the green Chesterfield, and sat down. As she sipped, she thought. She thought again about the colors of the wallpaper that might suit the baby's room, then about names again. Good English names: Caroline, Elizabeth, Charlotte, Victoria, Edward, William, Henry, and of course, Herbert Jr.

Yet soon, Lily Anne's thoughts settled uneasily on something odd her husband had suggested. Ever since he had made the suggestion a few days ago, she could not shake off how she felt about it—anxious, and yes— upset. She loved her husband, and indeed she had respect for that new doctor friend of his, so she had promised to consider it. But no, it was not what she wanted. She thought the scheme, which Herbert termed progressive and practical, was absurd, even unnatural!

The clock chimed in the hallway, infusing the pale light with a hollow cheer. Lily Anne took a deep breath and decided that men just don't understand things the way women do.

"I won't think even one more minute of the horrid idea," she said to herself. "I shall put it right out of my mind!"

She took a deep breath and another sip of tea as she stared a little blankly at the side table, where the sunlight twinkled off the crystal sherry decanter. For a moment, it seemed as if it was winking at her in solidarity. Lily Anne drank the rest of her tea. Then she pulled a ball of yellow yarn from the basket beside her feet and started to knit the baby's tiny socks.

With each stitch, she said to herself, "I must be strong."

Yes, in the late afternoon of that cello-sweet autumn, Lily Anne Kimble, despite the deep love she felt for her husband, vowed she would not agree to his outrageous idea. It was disturbing and far too risky. She would never let it happen.

CHAPTER 4

Mrs. Peterson looked at the kids around the supper table, then back down at her lasagna on the paper plate.

"Eat," she said, and Jason knew this word she said each evening was more command than invitation.

Her husband, Chuck Peterson, said nothing because he rarely spoke and simply nodded his head when his wife did. Jason dug into his precise eight ounces of lasagna, not focusing on anything but getting it down. The Petersons always ate from paper plates, the flimsy kind so that now the hot lasagna lifted some of the paper off and he swallowed it. He didn't enjoy mealtimes at the Petersons'. They were boring, a little scary, and always left him hungry.

Simon, who sat next to him, was three.

Now, Simon crowed, "Noodles!"

Across the table, five-year-old Alisha, the newest foster kid, smiled shyly at Simon and Jason.

"Tomorrow morning," Mrs. Peterson said to Jason, "your new caseworker, Ms. Opper, is coming over. She wants to talk to you about college."

"OK," Jason mumbled.

"Don't get your hopes up," Mrs. Peterson cautioned Jason, all the while looking at her husband. "We know from experience that foster kids rarely go to college. There's little tuition for it. Not a practical idea."

"Yeah," Jason mumbled. He'd figure out a way to get to MIT, money or not.

"Well, clean up," Chuck Peterson said when they'd finished eating.

The Petersons were the seventh foster family Jason had lived with since he was born. He'd lived with them for almost a year now, and it was OK. Not terrible. Not good.

They didn't care squat about him, but the "parents" here didn't beat him like they had in some other places and no one called him names, either. And yes, they snooped through his things, but he'd stopped caring about that. He didn't have much anyway, and he kept everything in one suitcase, so he wouldn't have to pack up for the next place. The other kids here were OK too, because there were only two of them, and they were so little, they couldn't mess with him or steal his stuff. The only thing he hated here was Mrs. Peterson. She had confiscated his soldering machine because she said it was dangerous. Bull! It was only when he hinted he'd tell social services about her restricting their food and watering down the powdered milk that she returned it. Shoot, if he couldn't have soldered those tiny computer components, how would he have brought his holograms to life?

After dinner, Jason loaded and ran the dishwasher, wiped the counters and scrubbed the baking dish and the pots, as those were his chores. Then he went up to his room and practiced the trumpet for his band class. He wasn't really interested in playing the trumpet, but he liked that the trumpet practice was a good excuse for not talking. Then, when everyone else went to bed, the house was quiet and he could think about things. Around ten, he went up to the bedroom he shared with Simon. Simon was asleep. Jason opened his backpack to take out his physics book, when he saw he'd accidentally brought with him Melanie's binder with her science report on ignition systems. Jason stretched out on the childish faded *Star Wars* comforter on his bed and read it, intrigued. He read it again. She was really something.

Toward midnight, Jason lay his head on the pillow, shaped by some other kid's head before him. As on so many other nights, he lay awake, and wondered who he was. After a while, he got up, slid downstairs and out into the backyard. He gazed up at the stars speckling the black sky, and as always, they appeared to him like tiny bits of some great broken mirror. As long as Jason could remember, he had sensed the stars held all the answers to the questions that we on Earth ask. Whenever he looked up into the night sky, the same, odd thought came to him. If he could just put enough of those celestial mirror pieces together, the hurt would stop, for they'd reflect back to him with the immense force of the cosmos—who he was.

CHAPTER 5

Carol Opper perched her slim body on the edge of the Petersons' plastic-covered recliner and shone her happy brown eyes on Jason.

"Absolutely fantastic!" she whooped. "When Mrs. Peterson told me you'd won first prize, I was so happy for you. Doors will open! I know *you* know that too." She winked at Jason. "And so, of course, Jason, I'd like to hear which universities you're thinking of?"

Because he had no family, Jason had had a lot of caseworkers in his life, and he had learned not to trust them. Sometimes, they could make the really bad things stop, but they couldn't ever make really good things happen. Now he sat beside Mr. and Mrs. Peterson on the long brown sofa and didn't answer, because her word "universities" took him by surprise.

Ms. Opper smiled as she said, "You don't need to be so modest!" She was young and upbeat, but Jason didn't dare believe she liked him, even though she was trying unsuccessfully to share her admiration for Jason with the Petersons. "You've accomplished a lot and you're sixteen now, Jason. It's time to think about college. The scholarship will open doors. And, if you win the Nevada competition, you'll be writing your own ticket to *anywhere*. So, what do you think?"

Jason sat silent while Mrs. Peterson looked at him with the fixed gaze of a reptile.

"As foster parents," she said, too loudly for indoors, "we've seen from experience that college is not a practical choice for a—"

"MIT . . . computer science and physics," Jason blurted, surprising even himself by speaking his heart's desire.

Mrs. Peterson, surprised by his interruption, let out a derisive chuckle.

"Massachusetts Institute of Technology," Ms. Opper said. "Excellent choice. Not easy to get into. Expensive too, but scholarships help, and I know that you've just won the first of several."

When he was reading about holograms at the library, Jason had read a lot of articles written by people at MIT. He knew at MIT, he could make his mark. He could advance the science of holography. He could dive into the really new stuff—futuristic stuff like deepfakes and digital twin technology, robotic machine learning for navigation, holographic optics, and SLAM. Yes, MIT was his dream think tank but did he, Jason, with few resources, no known last name, no family, no one who had ever *really* cared about him—did he dare hope he could get in?

On a late Saturday afternoon, Jason was heading out the door to the library to pick up a book for his optics research.

"Can I come?" Alisha asked.

Jason turned to look down at the little girl eagerly looking up at him. Her hair was combed and set in lots of braids.

"No, Alisha, you can't come."

"But I want to go with you," Alisha said.

"You can't."

"Why not?"

"I need to do what I need to do alone." Then Jason added, "Don't take it personally."

"What does *personally* mean?"

"Means there's nothing wrong with *you*," Jason answered, paused a moment, then said gently, "Wait here."

He ran upstairs, came back and handed her something rectangular, made of metal and smaller than a penny.

"A robot!" she squealed. "Thank you, Jason."

He had made the miniature robot by attaching tiny wires for arms and legs to an old cell phone memory chip, then painted a face on it.

"Bye, Alisha," he said. "See you later." Then he was out the door.

As he walked down Laurel Street, he wondered whether he should call Melanie.

He had never called a girl before.

In fact, he had just about never called anyone, because until just a few months ago, he didn't have a working phone, and besides, who would he call? After living in so many places, moving so many times, he was wary of trying to make friends that he'd just lose. Yet now, on this spring morning, Jason let his mind *think* of calling Melanie.

And of going to the prom with her. Melanie was not only pretty and smart, she was nice.

If he went to the prom with her, though, maybe she'd think he was her boyfriend. Well, he wasn't, but could he be? He pushed the idea away. Something within him made him not want to be close to people. He yearned for closeness, yet feared it too. If someone got to know him, they'd find him to be what he was, not only different, but worse—unlovable. No, he didn't want anyone thinking anything about him. He wouldn't call Melanie. He *couldn't.* He'd just think about her; that's what he'd do.

Jason was thinking about Melanie as he cut through Clearview City Park to the library. He was thinking how nice Melanie Sandersborn would look if she were dressed for a prom. Would she wear a long dress? Did all girls wear long dresses to the prom? He thought of her with her hair up atop her head and maybe a few soft curls floating down like little blackbird feathers.

He was thinking of Melanie so much, he didn't

notice the stranger who had been watching him from across the street and now called, "JASON. STOP! JASON! JASON, I NEED TO TALK WITH YOU!"

Jason did not even look at the man, for he knew he was the stranger. The *strange* stranger. The crazy one, who had tried to talk with him the other times. Like after school a few weeks ago, and again the following week and last week too. The guy was stalking him! He was the same guy who had sent him the letter he had thrown out unopened. Now Jason did what he'd done before, ignore him.

"Don't look!" he told himself. "Don't turn around!" Jason walked quickly on, despite the man calling his name, shouting for him to stop. How did he even know his name! Who *was* he?

Jason started to run. He ran through the park, where a maze of paths led through a dense grove of trees and he'd be hard to follow.

Deep inside the park, Jason calmed down, knowing he was out of sight of the stranger, and his thoughts returned to Melanie. He liked her laugh, which was as soft as a pigeon cooing, not a shriek like the laugh of some girls. And it was in that moment, thinking of her laugh, when Jason felt the tap on his shoulder. He spun around.

The man smiled at him. Just as Jason turned to run again, the guy, though old, reached out and firmly caught his arm.

"Jason, I just want to talk with you. Please listen to me. I've been trying to talk with you. I won't hurt you. Please believe me. I have things to tell you."

"Let go of me!"

"Please Jason, I need to talk with you! Can we talk somewhere? I've been trying to reach you for weeks, but I didn't have your email and you—"

"Whoever you are, leave me the hell alone!"

The man let go of Jason's arm, and for a moment, they stared at each other. Then Jason ran, fast through the park and out the other side. He left the man far behind, out of sight, and he knew the old guy couldn't catch up with him. His breath slowed as he walked toward the Clearview County Library and up the steps. Forcing himself to shut the man from his mind, he quickly found the book on computer programming he wanted, then he sat at the library's computer and found the listing for the book he needed most of all: *Optics:*

Interference and Diffraction by L.G. Barnwell, but it wasn't on the library shelf or checked out. Jason walked over to the woman sitting at the desk.

"I want to take this book out," he told her, handing her the paper scrap on which he had written the title.

"Well, let's see where it is," the librarian said, pushing her glasses farther up her nose as she entered the title into the computer and then after searching, said, "I'm afraid it's not available at our library."

"Can you order it for me?" Jason asked.

"It's just out and I'm afraid it's not available yet."

"But I need it. I need it for my research on holography. You see, I can't afford it and . . . well, when could you get it in?"

"I'm sorry," the woman said quietly. "It's not in circulation yet, and I don't know when precisely it will be."

Jason turned from her and walked out of the library. He needed that book, and when he had looked at the price of it on Amazon, it was about a hundred and thirty dollars, and he didn't have that kind of money. In frustration, he kicked the library's steel drop-off box so hard, he hurt his toe.

I need to chill out, he thought. The crazy guy and this library book disappointment unnerved him. Jason walked the three blocks to Tom's Coffee Shop, went in and sat at the counter. He was hungry now, and with what he had left from his small allowance, he could buy the Saturday special: spaghetti and meatballs. And that'd be a good thing because then he could tell Mrs. Peterson he'd already eaten and wouldn't have to sit at supper with them and watch Mrs. Peterson portion out the mean amounts of food on each plate. But when he opened his wallet to check his money, he saw he had less than he'd thought. Two dollars. Just enough for just a glass of milk, so he ordered that.

After he ordered, he pulled out the computer book from his backpack and had read the first sentences when someone slid onto the stool next to him.

The stranger.

"Jason, I'm not going to hurt you," the man said. "Just want to talk with you." Without looking at him, Jason muttered, "How do you know my name?"

"I just do, and I have important things to tell you." He dropped a card into Jason's open backpack. "My name's Roy. Roy Calvert."

Jason said nothing.

"We could talk, meet and I'll lend you that book you want, *Optics: Interference and Diffraction.*"

"How did you know about the book? You've been following me, haven't you?"

"I'll give you the book and we can talk."

"Look, old man, I'm not going to your house. Not now. Not ever. I'll stay right where I am." Jason's words sounded to him like those of some guy in a Western.

The man named Roy stroked his bald head, while saying, "You don't have to come to my house. I'll give it to you tomorrow. We can meet here or anywhere."

Jason stared at the man, sizing him up. The offer was absurd. How could the man get the book that fast, even if he ordered it online? And it was too much of a coincidence that the guy would have had just the book he wanted. Jason felt that panicky feeling again. He grabbed his computer book from the counter, stood up, and rushed out of the coffee shop.

All the next day, Jason's thoughts kept returning to the book. How, he thought, could the man do him harm if they met in front of the coffee shop or the library or anywhere *public*? Jason needed that book. At last, he made up his mind. He dug inside his backpack and pulled out Roy's card. But the card had no email address nor phone number. Just the name "Roy Calvert" and a street address, which Jason Googled and saw that it was about ten miles east—in the suburbs, a twenty-five-minute bus ride. Well, that was it. With no other way to contact him, he had to go there.

Jason walked up the cement path of Roy's house, past the front yard, landscaped with cactus. On the bus over here, he went over in his mind what he'd do and *not* do. He stopped at the brown front door with the bright brass knocker and he felt again inside his jeans pocket for the pocketknife he always kept with him. If the man proved to be a creep, a pedophile, a psycho, Jason would draw out that knife and he'd sure use it. He pressed the doorbell.

"Jason," Roy said with a smile when he opened the door. "It's a wonder you're here, and you yourself are a wonder." He added with a slight chuckle, "As I guess I am too."

"I came for the book."

"It's downstairs," Roy answered. "I'll get it." He disappeared for a few minutes, while Jason stood at the threshold, hearing the mingled sounds of kids playing across the street and the neighborly groan of a lawn mower. When Roy came back, he handed the book to Jason. "You can keep it. I don't need it anymore." Jason stuffed the book in his backpack.

"Thanks," he mumbled.

"I've got lunch almost ready," Roy said.

"I'm not staying."

"You must be hungry."

Jason was hungry. He hadn't eaten dinner the night before because he couldn't face Mrs. Peterson talking to him about practicality. He'd had nothing but a slice of toast for breakfast. Now, from the doorway, he smelled something good cooking and his stomach rumbled. He knew it was wrong to enter a stranger's house. No, not just wrong. Stupid. Dangerous.

But in a moment Jason rationalized, "I've got my knife, and I'm sure stronger than this old codger."

He entered the house and got a good smell of the place. It didn't smell like a house; it smelled like *a home.* Jason had lived in so many places, he had become expert at casing out a new one, so within seconds, he figured out a lot. The man was not poor, for the carpet felt thick and cushiony under his shoes. And the place was clean; there was a fresh pine smell, not from a pine-scented disinfectant but from pine wood. And the good cooking smell. Also, he saw the guy liked to read, for floor-to-ceiling rows of books lined one wall and a pile of books teetered on the coffee table. Soon after entering, there sounded the stately chime of a large wooden wall clock.

Jason stood in the living room and looked beyond to the kitchen, which was all sparkle and cheer. He took in the white counters, mirror bright toaster, and against the yellow wall, he caught the gleam of stainless steel pots lined up on a shelf.

He followed Roy Calvert into the kitchen and sat in the chair Roy pointed to. Jason felt edgy though. Jumpy. It was one thing to talk to a stranger in a public place and another thing to go to a stranger's house, and yet another thing to enter that house and eat there. He wondered who the guy was. And he wondered why he'd come inside when he knew he shouldn't have. The situation felt weird. Yet it was when the man placed his meal in front of him, that the situation got even weirder and Jason had another thing to wonder about.

CHAPTER 6

IT WAS A CLEAR WINTER NIGHT WHEN LILY ANNE Kimble walked up the icy metal steps and onto the plane.

"Welcome aboard," the stewardess greeted her. "May I take your wrap?"

Lily Anne, wearing the silver fox jacket Herbert had given her for their fifth anniversary, removed it and handed it to the young lady.

"Thank you," she said with a smile. She went to the seat the lady pointed to and sat down beside the little round window. Herbert took the seat next to her. Lily Annie removed her gloves and shut them up in her brown leather handbag.

On that cold bright night, Lily Anne felt as giddy as a schoolgirl. After the days of worry and doubt, she now felt liberated. Her husband was a rock, just what she needed. His idea, which only days ago had seemed to her abhorrent, now seemed sensible, indeed necessary. Why had she fretted so? Hadn't she dreamed of performing in the great concert halls of London, Amsterdam, and Vienna? And now, she, Lily Anne Kimble, was not only going to be the premier performer at concerts in these great cities and many more, but she was also going to achieve her lifelong dream to see the world.

"It's now or never for you, dear," her husband had warned, and at last she had come to see that he was right. After all, she would give birth right after she returned. She was only thirty, so what was a delay of a year? Nothing! As that nice scientist, Doctor Ernst Fritzhauer had said, "It's a modern career decision." Traveling freely with Herbert, she would become, in the next twenty-four months, a world-renowned concert cellist. Yes, she would be famous, her international career assured.

The stewardess handed them glasses of champagne, and as she sipped hers, smiling at her husband, she patted her now flat stomach and thought dreamily of her future children. Now that they lay in what Dr. Fritzhauer called a "suspended-animation state," Lily

Anne thought of them as napping in a kind of fluid cradle. Yes. She liked to think of the situation just like that, and she liked to think of the gifts she would buy: little hand-stitched nightgowns in Paris, lace bonnets in Italy, a puppet in Germany, and oh—all manner of toys!

The engine noise grew louder. Herbert planted a kiss on Lily Anne's lightly-powdered cheek and whispered in her ear, "My darling, we're on our way!"

Lily Anne felt a thrill like a little surge of electricity run through her. She giggled and kissed his cheek, then they both turned toward the window as the plane thundered down the runway and lifted into the night. They stared out the window, but of course with the light in the cabin, there was nothing to see but their own faces reflected. As the plane roared upward, Lily Anne was struck by a sudden panic. Before she had left the house this morning, she'd meant to send off that confidential letter to her sister in England . . . just in case something happened. But now she realized that, in her rush to pack and check everything, she had forgotten to put it in the mailbox! That most important letter was still on the entryway table. "NO!" Lily Anne thought in anguish, "PLEASE GOD, NO!"

CHAPTER 7

JASON LOOKED DOWN TO SEE, ON A SNOW-WHITE PLATE in front of him, a mound of spaghetti with six meatballs. Roy placed a tall glass of root beer above the left side of his plate and Jason wondered how Roy knew he was left-handed. The root beer had a dash of milk floating on the top. It was his dream meal. How did Roy know this?

Jason stared at the food, surprised but not shocked. After all, he knew grownups mess with your head. Grownups were phonies and bullies. He hesitated for a moment. Should he even eat this food? The old fart could be a psychopath and the food poisoned. But something within Jason told him the guy was just eccentric, so he dug in.

Roy sat down in the opposite chair with the same

meal and drink for himself.

"Well, Jason," he said, "as I told you, my name's Roy Calvert. And I say it's about time we met, as we've got a lot to talk about, to learn and to do together."

Jason said nothing because he didn't know what the guy meant. He looked up at the man, as if seeing him for the first time.

Roy was bald, his lower head rimmed with wisps of gray hair, light as dust. His green eyes were like Jason's, only paler, as if faded with age. His round face was wrinkled burlap, and his jaws slack as a hound's.

"You're really old," Jason thought, then realized he'd said it aloud.

Roy smiled. "Only seventy-three."

"Who are you?" Jason asked.

Solemnly, the hall clock struck three.

As if on cue, Roy spoke. He spoke earnestly, as if he were telling the most important news of the millennium. He said how long he had tried to find Jason, and when after years, he did, how he had wanted to contact Jason directly, not through his foster parents. And by God, Jason and he needed to get to know each other!

Jason listened to him, but what the man was saying made no sense, so after a few moments, he listened no differently than he listened to other adults—which was hardly at all and with concealed contempt. He had learned that most grownups don't really care about you, and many hurt you. With this attitude, he caught only bits of the story, for suddenly he didn't care who the man was. Jason had already put the book in his backpack, so when he'd finished the last bite of food, he'd be gone. He was not going to let himself endure more boring ramble.

"But things didn't turn out as they wished," Roy was saying, then he paused. His lower lip trembled just a bit as he looked at Jason, trying to make eye contact. "Jason, you probably know that thrust is generated by the propulsion system of an airplane, usually through some application of Newton's Second Law, so that . . ."

"*Third*," muttered Jason.

"I stand corrected. *Third* Law. Well, they knew this back then, but they may not have been too clear on how engine air can get lost mid-flight and drastically reduce thrust, so somewhere over the Atlantic, the plane decelerated below the speed at which directional control could be maintained and spiraled toward the sea."

Jason stuck the last strands of spaghetti into his mouth. He was looking at the geezer's arms. They were surprisingly muscular. Pretty strong for someone so old.

". . . all they bequeathed was the icy-pain of loneliness."

Suddenly, Roy stopped. He looked Jason in the eyes. Jason quickly looked down at his plate.

"Listen, Jason. *Listen.* What I'm about to tell you is not about people long gone or biology. It's about identity and kinship, which can be hidden or fragmented like pieces of a mirror."

Jason had not been paying attention but when he caught the words "fragmented like pieces of a mirror," he leaned in. How surprising, how mysterious it was that Roy would think of identity like that.

Roy went on. "It's about love and the need for . . ."

When Jason heard the word "love," it was like a stab of pain and suddenly he felt he wanted to leave.

"Thanks for the spaghetti," he said nervously as he stood up, "but I can't follow your story."

Roy swept his hand slowly over his thin hair a few times as if petting a dog, then he stood up too, so that now they stood facing each other across the kitchen table.

"What I have to tell you, Jason, is going to save me, and it's going to save you too. I know you're cynical. Me too. I was cynical as a sinner. And I suspect you've been hurt, but you need to calm yourself and let me explain. There's important stuff you need to know. I don't mean to scare you. I mean to help you." He moved closer to Jason. "To help you piece together the fragments . . ."

Roy moved closer to him, and to Jason, it was too close. His defensive instincts from his beatings kicked in. Without thinking, he swung at Roy and hit him on the jaw, harder than he wanted to. He heard a sound like twigs cracking. Roy toppled over onto the linoleum floor, where he lay. Still as a corpse.

I killed him, Jason thought in panic. *No time to think! Need to go!* He grabbed his backpack off the kitchen counter and ran to the door.

But in his panic, he got disoriented and ran not toward the front door, but the door of some room.

Recognizing his mistake, he would simply have had to turn around and head out in the other direction—out the front door, out to freedom.

But he didn't.

Instead, Jason stood in the dim light of that room, shocked into stillness by what he saw.

CHAPTER 8

IT WAS A SMALL ROOM, USED AS A KIND OF OFFICE WITH a big oak desk, a black leather armchair, and a beige carpet. A framed poster of the solar system and a landscape painting hung on one wall above the desk. On the opposite wall, above a low bookcase, hung framed black-and-white photos, including three of *himself.* One when he was about thirteen, another when he was about eight or nine, and a black and white photo of him when he was little, maybe five. Jason stared, transfixed. He had never seen himself in any family album or in anyone's wallet, or in a frame on anyone's desk, fridge, mantel, or wall. He had never seen a picture of just himself. Yet in this stranger's house, there were pictures of him, and they were displayed!

He had struggled to suppress his childhood, not remember all the hurt, but now it seemed pieces of his childhood were *here.* The photo of him when he was really young showed him in suspenders and shorts; he didn't remember those clothes, but he did remember *himself.* He noted the little hammer-shaped birthmark on his arm. The adults in the photos looked strange. But he was so young in the picture, and over the years, he'd blanked out the bad grown-ups from his mind. He looked at the photo again and his eyes fell on the date written on it.

"I didn't mean to scare you. I realize now I scared you."

Jason spun round. Roy stood pale in the doorway with a bloody gash on his cheek. Despite his injury, he looked calm.

"I didn't mean to scare you," he repeated. "I'm sorry."

Jason ran forward, pushed him aside, and bolted out of the house. He ran like a crazed animal, as if the old man were chasing him, but Roy was not chasing him. Jason had left him far behind, yet he kept on running, not thinking how to get back to the Petersons', or even if he was running in the right direction. It was only after twenty minutes or so that he stopped, collapsing on the ground, fighting hard to get his breath, feeling like someone was choking him. After a little while, he felt his breath grow regular, and when it did, he realized what he was escaping *from.* Not just from the demented old codger, but from the burning-fire mystery of those photos! What were they doing on his wall? Who took them? When? *Why?* Something else even weirder too . . . what was it?

What? There was an odd fact about those photos. A glimpse of something not correct. What was it? *What?* Jason's mind was a merry-go-round. He gripped his head in his hands as if he could force his frantic mind to stop whirling. *Stop!* he warned himself, *Stop! Think of IMPORTANT THINGS! I need to think about where I am right now. I need to get back to the Peterson house.* The Petersons! Were they wondering where he was? Did they care?

NO! OF COURSE THEY DON'T! he scolded himself. *Don't ever think of who cares about you. Never think of that!*

Only when Jason boarded the bus did he see he was

sixty-four cents short of the fare back to Clearview.

"Sorry, son," the driver said.

Jason descended from the bus and hurried along the highway. He came to a sign that read, "Clearview: 8 Miles." Knowing he was moving in the right direction, he kept walking. It'd take him a couple of hours, maybe longer, but he'd get there. The sky darkened, then came rain. As he walked, his shoulder ached from the violence. Rain soaked his clothes and hurt soaked his heart. But now in the cold and wet, as in bad times before, he forced himself not to think about what hurt.

CHAPTER 9
May 2025

A MONTH LATER, JASON WAS PLACED IN A NEW FOSTER home. Ms. Opper told him the Petersons wanted to quit foster parenting, so he had to move on—to the Kramers. He told himself he didn't care a dog's butt either way.

The Kramers were new at foster parenting and trying to be good at it. Jason was their first and only kid, and they wanted it to work. They lived in a small, tidy house on Cedar Street, just a few blocks from the Petersons. Their house was cheerful—with big windows and vases of the roses Mrs. Kramer grew placed all about. Mr. and Mrs. Kramer called each other "Honey" and "Sweetie" and weren't embarrassed by it. For years, they had wanted to have a baby of their own, but couldn't. They turned to adoption but that hadn't worked out for them, and now they were told they were too old to adopt a baby, so they'd decided to try foster parenting. Somehow, Ms. Opper got them to try a teenager first.

The Kramers were doing their best—buying Jason a new smartphone, paying for a data package, paying for driving lessons and even promising him a car, if and when he got his license. Mr. Kramer even let Jason drive an old motorcycle he had around the block a couple of times.

When he was little in those hellish homes, Jason would have responded to the Kramers' caring. Not now. He knew the score too well. He'd be out of the foster care system forever in a year and he'd never see them again and they sure wouldn't give a thought to him once he was gone and another kid moved in.

At the Kramers', Jason had his own room for the first time in his life. It was a large bedroom with a window that looked out onto a grassy backyard. They told him the room was his as long as he was with them. Jason mumbled thanks for the things there he liked: sleeping on new sheets that were just for him and even having his own bathroom. He took down the dumb football pennants they'd put up for him in his room and taped up his optics charts and trigonometry diagrams.

In October, Jason won the Nevada Science Competition for his research. Now he had two scholarships and was on fire to do much more. It was like he could taste MIT now. He stayed up long nights reading science articles, and he learned a lot of new things about holograms, optical illusions, and virtual reality. If he kept at it, he knew he could figure out how to control his illusions better. He didn't want his holograms running amok like they had in the gym. He needed to learn how to precisely program them, make them life-size, and be able to produce them *instantly* with realistic sound. If he could do those things, then he would have done what no one else before him had. He'd put his mark on holography. He'd make applications to benefit medicine and save people's lives, and by doing that, he'd let others know who he really was—not a pathetic orphan or foster kid, but a researcher, an expert, a scientist. And, in some way, this would save his own life. He'd no longer feel he didn't belong to anything, for he would belong to science.

As the weeks rolled on, Jason settled into the

Kramers' house. They fed him well—no rationing. He could eat whatever he wanted from the cupboard, whenever he wanted it. They even took him to the mall and bought him computer programming books and clothes.

"Pick out what you like Jason. *You'll* be wearing them so pick out what you like."

It was the first time anyone had paid from their own pocket for *new* clothes for him. Good new clothes too. Expensive stuff. They gave him a gift card so he could buy books and music. That was something new too. They didn't mind his soldering machine or tell him what time he had to turn the lights out. Yet the Kramers asked him too many questions: What did he like to read? What did he like to wear? What did he like to eat? It was like being pummeled. Why were they always prying? Did regular kids' parents do that?

Parents. When he even thought of that word, he felt a swift stab of sorrow.

Maybe the Kramers were acting nice because they *were* nice. Which didn't mean they liked him. He knew that well enough. No one ever really *liked* him, even when he was little and maybe almost lovable then.

Jason knew that, when they got to know him better, the Kramers would see how abnormal he was. It was just a matter of time.

Time he didn't intend to waste. Each evening, he escaped to his room, where he pored over the programming books and books on virtual reality, animation, and optics.

He read Roy's book three times and made copious notes. He bought old smartphones cheap online, took them apart and, with the eyebrow tweezers he had swiped from Mrs. Kramer, he reprogrammed them with new, powerful capabilities. He could now make life-size holograms and make them faster, almost instantly. He also learned more about SLAM (simultaneous localization and mapping), which would help him manage them better, really control their every movement.

Soon, it was December of his senior year, and the Kramers made him take a photo with them.

"For the family holiday card," Mrs. Kramer said.

Jason studied the photo, realizing with surprise that, at seventeen, he'd grown taller. *Tall.* He had to admit, in those long moments of staring into the bathroom mirror, that now with his new stature and curly brown hair, he *looked* like a college student.

The acceptance letter from MIT came as a surprise. Carol Opper had helped him apply and, for his essay, persuaded him to write how he'd struggled with being an orphan. Jason knew that this bleeding-heart essay Ms. Opper suggested had boosted his chance of getting an acceptance, but he was surprised by the four-year scholarship that went with it. And even more surprised when he learned that Melanie too would be attending MIT to major in Electrical Science and Engineering. Melanie at MIT! The idea made him both nervous and happy and full of emotions he didn't understand.

The letter said Jason could begin attending in June of next year. He thought about what it would be like to go off to college. He couldn't wait to get there, where he'd be free and he'd have all the resources to advance his research. And maybe he'd get up the courage there to talk to Melanie, *take her on a date.*

Yet, as the weeks marched toward graduation, Jason found himself thinking less about college or holograms or even about Melanie Sandersborn. In the quiet of his room at night, Jason's mind traveled back to Roy Calvert—to those photos of himself that remained impossible to explain by any law of science. And, to the mysterious fact of those photos in Roy's room that had floated back to him, haunting him with its illogic. The date he'd seen on one of those photos of himself was 1960—*forty-nine years before he was born. How was that possible?*

And then there were those words, the only words he had remembered the guy speaking—*Identity and kinship can be hidden or fragmented like pieces of a mirror.* That's what Jason had sensed his whole life—his identity was hidden. But if, as Jason knew, the universe contains everything that we know exists, then maybe Roy Calvert, loony old guy that he was, really might somehow be able to do what he said—*piece together the fragments* to give Jason the thing he most yearned for: identity.

Finally, he couldn't stand that nagging feeling anymore. On a late and blustery spring afternoon, two weeks before he was due to leave Clearview forever, Jason walked out of the Kramer house and caught the bus heading east. It was twilight when he got off and his mind swirled with the questions he'd ask.

He made his way past the long tree-shaded streets until he came to the sand-colored rancher with the dark brown trim. He went up the cement path, and before he could put his finger to the doorbell, the door swung open.

"Come on in," Roy said, "I was expecting you."

CHAPTER 10

June 4, 2026

"You're just in time," Roy said.

Jason looked at him in surprise. "For what?"

"Supper."

"I came to see you about something."

"Of course you did," Roy said. "Why else would you be here? Criminy! Almost forgot . . . need to back up something on the computer. C'mon."

Jason followed Roy through the kitchen and down the narrow stairs to the basement. Roy flicked on the light and Jason saw the basement was a really large room—part laboratory, part workshop. Crammed with telescopes, microscopes test tubes, mirrors, lenses, bottles of chemicals. One whole wall held floor-to-ceiling books, hundreds of them—like the guy had his own library. Another wall held shelves of metal and wood scraps, nails, screws, wires, bolts and machine parts, but it was the third wall that stunned him. On that wall, a real supercomputer stood, big as a refrigerator and next to it three monitors, each wide as a flat screen TV. Roy walked over to the computer and closed some files.

"Wow!" Jason exclaimed.

"Nice, isn't it? I do a fair amount of puttering down here."

Jason stared in awe at the super-powerful computer he'd thought existed only at certain universities.

"The computer," Roy said, "is an odd animal. Talks. Doesn't walk. Gets educated by humans, then mimics them. Gets sick. Shuts down. Pretends to sleep."

"It's a beauty," Jason breathed.

"Bet your buttons it is! I have a shameful amount of fun with it."

"Fun?"

"Like this." Roy walked over to the computer, entered something, then switched off the lights. At once, the basement ceiling was transformed into the night sky. Slowly, it shifted from the northern hemisphere sky to the southern one.

Jason drew in a gasp. "You've got your own planetarium!"

"Well, I used to be an optical engineer, using computers to design lenses for contraptions like telescopes, and maybe that's why I think it's a worthy thing to look at stars. You can learn a lot by looking at them: the age of the universe, its life expectancy, and all kinds of things about yourself."

Jason stared at Roy in surprise. That was what *he* had always suspected. He wondered what Roy would think of his thought that the stars might somehow be able to tell him who he was. He'd never tell Roy, though. It would sound crazy.

As if reading his mind, Roy added, "Of course, why shouldn't the stars tell us about ourselves? The carbon, nitrogen, and oxygen atoms in our bodies were created more than 4.5 billion years ago by stars. And because we contain these elements, we're made of stars." Roy stopped, as if awed by his own words, then flipped the lights back on.

"I like stars too," Jason said quietly. "I mean I like science and I've been experimenting with optics, reflection, vision, holograms—stuff like that."

"Stuff like what?"

"Well," Jason said slowly, "I figured out a way to immediately create a hologram from a photo, even a torn one or many bits of one. I figured out mathematically the way each piece could hold the whole image and how to program the image to behave realistically. I made a program to do this when I was a junior, but I've been working on improving that program. I want to control holograms better, so a hologram can contain way more information than they do now. To be able to make human-size holograms from my phone and make these illusions higher quality and faster—on the fly. And I want to make other illusions, too—cars, bicycles, scooters, and other moving objects—capture their movement and appearance, like in a movie but in 3D. To do that, I need to be able to project a full color hologram, but that means I need about a hundred and fifty million computations per second and I don't have all the . . ."

"Programming know-how," Roy said.

Jason stared at him. "How did you know?"

"How could I *not* know?"

They looked at each other.

"Let's figure it out," Roy said.

A couple of hours passed, in which Jason brought his backpack down to the basement and pulled from it the program description for his *Hyper-Hologram* idea. Roy studied it and then looked at Jason's computer code.

"Your code's too complicated. Like a good hamburger, simpler's better. You don't need to write fancy code to get what you want. Write simple, clear stuff."

Roy showed Jason how to rewrite the programming code. Jason saw that Roy knew what he was doing. Together, they worked on calculating the refraction of the light with the distance needed. Their goal was to develop a program that would coordinate all Jason's new scientific formulations on the device. As they worked, they discussed the formulations, argued, talked some more, even joked a couple of times. For the first time in his life, Jason felt he had found someone he could talk with, someone who might understand him. Roy still used handkerchiefs and CDs, yet he was someone who asked the same questions Jason asked and was intrigued by the same things. Someone like a friend.

By the time the two realized they were hungry, they also realized night had come.

"Let's eat," Roy said.

Jason packed the programming papers back into his backpack. "I'd like to see the stars again," he said.

Roy went back to the computer, and in moments, a starry sky hung over them.

Jason gazed upward. "I like stars," he said softly. "I look at them a lot and I wonder what they mean." Jason paused but then went on, suddenly not caring what dumbass thing he revealed about himself. "I sometimes think the stars can tell us something, mean something for us . . . I mean . . . for *me*."

There. He had done it. Maybe because it's easier to say things in the dark, he had told his most heartfelt thought to somebody.

"Stars might well mean something," Roy agreed. "I believe the universe holds information for us, and if we don't receive the information, it's because we haven't worked hard enough to darn well learn it. At any rate, I like looking up into the night sky—I'm not talking about my ceiling, but the real one. Whenever I wonder where I came from and who I am and why I'm here, I feel somehow the stars are guides to the answers. It's not science, it's a sense. Perhaps it works by just the fact the stars are so many and stretch so far and are so pretty, that they invite big questions and just asking questions is halfway to answering them."

Jason didn't quite know what Roy meant but it sounded right somehow.

As Roy flipped the hamburgers in the cast iron pan, Jason decided he would ask the questions he had come to ask, as soon as they'd finished dinner.

Pick the right time to bring it up, he reminded himself. *Don't rush things.*

CHAPTER II

July 2022
Carson City, Nevada

THE MAN STEPPED OUT OF HIS CAR AND WALKED across the wide plaza, heading for the nineteenth-century state capitol with its Greek pillars and great domed roof. The intense summer heat struck him like a lightning bolt, and as he walked, he felt slightly faint but he kept on. He stroked the fine wisps of gray hair atop his near-bald head and berated himself for not wearing a hat.

On entering the impressive brick building, he stood for a moment in awe of the polished marble floor, grand staircase, and long walls with oil portraits of famous Nevadans, of whom he knew nothing. Then he walked to the directory on the wall and, locating the Recorder's Office, headed for it.

The office was surprisingly small. A young woman sat at a desk facing the door.

"May I help you?" she asked.

"I'd like to sit," the man said.

"Please," the woman said, gesturing to the chair in front of her desk.

With the back of his hand, he wiped the sweat from his forehead. "I'm looking for a family member," he said, and as he was out of breath, his voice came out louder than he wanted.

"We have an online registry and a public-use computer right here, if you'd like to do a search."

"I already searched online," the man said. "Found nothing."

Not taking her eyes off her computer screen, the woman asked, "Are you looking for someone before 1856?"

"No. I am looking for someone born on May 22, 2009, to a woman named Rachel Bennington."

"In Nevada?"

"Yes. In Nevada. But I found nothing."

"By any chance, was this person born in 2009 adopted?"

"Yes."

"Then you need to know, sir, that if you've had no luck finding this person, it could very well mean that it was a confidential adoption. In that case, there would be no birth record available."

"But couldn't a close relative view it?"

"No. What I'm saying to you is that this is what we call a 'closed adoption,' where we are provided with no record of it. No record of this person's birth would exist. Additionally, often in these types of adoption, there is no mother's or father's name recorded anywhere."

"Anywhere at all?" the man asked. "What about the Nevada State Department of Vital Statistics?"

"Anywhere at all," the woman repeated before turning back to her computer screen.

The man sat thinking for a moment, then slowly rose.

"Thank you," he mumbled as he walked out.

He walked down the steps in the blazing heat and to his car. He opened the door, slid into the driver's seat, rested his head against the hot steering wheel and wept.

CHAPTER 12

"Choose your weapons." Roy handed him the knives and forks.

Jason put the knives and forks on the table, then grabbed two napkins off the counter and put those out too. When he did this, the memory of his last "visit" flooded him. He remembered how scared he'd been, and his wild panic. Now he didn't feel scared. Traveling here on the bus, he'd told himself that, whatever happened, he was strong and could take care of himself. Either Roy had the information he wanted or he didn't.

"Sit yourself down." Roy gestured toward a chair at the table.

When Jason sat, he was reminded how Roy used placemats, clean ones like the Kramers used. Roy placed on his mat a plate with a big hamburger, corn on the cob, and a salad with ranch dressing and grated carrots all over the top, the way Jason liked it. How did Roy know?

Jason didn't wait for Roy, just hungrily began to eat, for this time, too, Roy had made all the food he most liked.

Roy poured coffee for himself and handed Jason a glass of root beer topped with milk. He sat down with his own plate, exactly the same. The two ate in silence.

After swallowing his last bite of hamburger, Jason said, "Why do you have those photos of me?"

Roy put his hamburger back on his plate. "What are you talking about?"

"The *photos*—in that room back there."

"Those aren't photos of you."

"What are you saying? Do you think I don't know my own face?"

"They are not photos of you."

"You know they are, so stop messing with me. They're photos of me, and I want to know why one has an old date on it: 1960. What's up with that?"

Roy looked at Jason steadily; then, after what felt like too long a time, he took a deep breath and said,

"No, Jason, they are not photos of you. They are photos of me."

After this joke, Jason looked hard at Roy, who looked right back at him.

"I'll explain it. You'll understand."

Roy poured more root beer into his glass and began explaining.

"I was adopted. My adoptive mother, Claire, was a typing teacher. My dad, Burt Calvert, was a family doctor, so he wanted me to be educated too. Being a doctor, he loved science and passed that love on to me. We lived in Ithaca, New York, then, and I won a lot of awards in high school and in the county, and once when I was fifteen, a statewide science contest for my 'talking robot.' It'd be considered pretty primitive nowadays, but I was on to something and worked with computers in the early days, when they were bigger than refrigerators. The Calverts were moral people, yet unable to give affection. I never felt loved by them, just taken care of, and without love, I felt lonely growing up . . . alone."

Roy's tale of his lonely childhood struck a nerve, making Jason uncomfortable.

"I don't see where this is going," he said. "Could you please just get to the point. Do you know who my parents were? Are you related to me somehow?"

"I'm getting to it, so put your mouth in neutral and *listen.* In 1976, my adoptive mother died of a stroke."

As Roy talked, Jason felt his anger flare. Roy had made a preposterous statement about those photos, a *lie,* and now, just like last time, was rambling on with pointless nostalgia!

"Where's this going?" Jason asked. "And what does it have to do with me?"

"Everything. My dad died in 2012 at the ripe old age of ninety-four, so we were grownups together for a good long while. I respected him but we weren't close. Whenever I'd ask about my biological parents, he'd say, 'We don't rightly know; we heard they were fine people.' Because I never got any real information, I figured there was something secret they didn't want me to know."

"I still don't see what this has to do with *me,*" Jason said, his voice louder as the anger inside him grew. "It's not that interesting to me."

"A lot of things aren't interesting until they get

interesting. Now, here's where *you* come in. When my dad died, his will left me some documents that held the answer to their silence. My father left a packet of documents with an attorney. These documents were to be entrusted to me ten years after his death. When I finally received them in 2022, I learned something shocking from a letter my father wrote for me. I was born *after* my biological mother and father died."

"That's impossible!" Jason hooted. "You can be born after your father dies but not after *your mother* dies! That's crap! Sounds like lousy science fiction."

"Sure does, and what I'm about to tell you will sound even more like science fiction. It may not sit well with you, but here it is: My dad had a patient named Mrs. Lily Anne Kimble. Lily Anne was a concert cellist, who had planned to launch her international career with a year-long world tour, playing in all the capital cities of the globe. Yet weeks before the trip, Lily Anne learned she was pregnant and with twins! A colleague of my father, a Dr. Ernst Fritzhauer, proposed that he could remove her embryos, and using a new but untried medical technique, preserve them by freezing them for two years until she returned. Then she would be implanted with the embryos and her pregnancy would proceed as normal. The letter said that her husband, my biological father, encouraged her in the plan and at last she consented.

"But things went wrong. Lily Anne and her husband were killed in a plane crash over the Atlantic. My adoptive dad must have been guilt-stricken to learn there were two babies that would never be born. Especially since he was the one who had suggested this ill-fated plan. So, he tried to persuade my mother to become pregnant with the Kimble embryos. They were childless, and this would have been the answer they had prayed for. He asked Dr. Fritzhauer for the embryos and Dr. Fritzhauer gave them to my dad.

"But there was a problem. My adoptive mother agreed, but as she was already in middle age, she agreed to bear just one—me."

"What did your dad do with the other one?" Jason asked.

Roy took a deep breath and another long sip of coffee. "Kept it. Like I said, my dad understood science, so he kept it in liquid nitrogen below three hundred twenty-one degrees Fahrenheit until 2009."

"Fifty-nine years!" Jason exclaimed.

"He couldn't bear to destroy it. Maybe he felt like he would be destroying another *me*. And he couldn't bear to tell me about it either. I often think how much he must have suffered with his long, lonely secret."

Roy now looked like he himself was suffering. When he cleared his throat, it sounded more like stifling a cry.

He wiped his glasses and then his eyes with a handkerchief pulled from his pocket and continued, "In conversation with a young doctor just a year before he died, he was told of a woman who wanted to bear her own child but could not. My father allowed him to take the second embryo and the doctor arranged for it to be implanted in this woman. Her name was Rachel Bennington. She was a single woman with money, thirty-five years old, and yearning for a child. On May 22, 2009, Rachel gave birth in her home with the doctor attending, but it turned out she had a weak heart and she died in childbirth."

Jason looked down at the table. He didn't want to hear the rest. It was too crazy. Bizarre!

"Now, Jason, listen up. That doctor wanted to know

for sure that the baby was my twin brother, so DNA testing was done. The test showed we were twin brothers and not just—"

"SHUT UP!" Jason shouted.

He was trembling a little now and his mind reeled. He had made a big effort—no—a *brave* effort to come here. Yet, in the last few hours, he had even dared hope that maybe he'd at last found someone he could talk with about things. But above all, he had come here because he had hoped he'd get an answer or at least a clue to his identity. Maybe old Roy knew something about some relative or something—*anything* that could connect him or just guide him. Now he saw his hopes destroyed in the face of Roy's insanity. The hogwash Roy was spewing branded him as nuts.

Roy paused at Jason's outburst, then continued earnestly. "When I learned about you, I wanted more than anything to find you—to tell you who you are, to know you and for you to know me. I searched for you by every means but I had no name for you and even if I had, your birth record was sealed. After more than five years of research and two years after my wife died, I got a clue from the Nevada Social Services . . ." Roy paused, took a breath and said, "And then, about a year ago, after petitioning the state for years, I finally received a file with a single document, dated May 24, 2009, citing a two-day-old baby boy put into their custody and now living with a family less than fifteen miles from me." Roy stopped, then said in a low voice, "I knew it was you."

Jason's trembling became stronger. Worse, he felt that sharp yearning he no longer wanted. The crazy man's words pierced his heart. *That* was what he had always wanted. To *belong.* To have a brother. Family! To love and be loved, like throwing a ball back and forth to someone and both catching it. He had wanted family, even if family meant only one person. But wanting something badly was a loser's game that long ago he had learned to stop playing.

"This is not your always home, Jason, but only until you are five."

"This, Jason, will be your family until you are seven."

"Now, Jason, you'll be living with the McWitters until you are ten."

"Think of the Kramers as your mom and dad until

you go to college."

"What are you thinking?" Roy asked.

"Temporary," Jason said.

"What?"

"You. *You* are temporary. You're old. You're so old, your time is almost up. You have maybe ten more years, then you'll be dead. Gone. *Temporary.* That's what you are. Won't matter to you or me or anyone else, because you're cracked. Knew it the first time and I was stupid to come back. You're crazy!' He did not see the sorrow on Roy's face, for now Jason's anger was rage. "Your whole story is crazy!"

Roy nodded, saying quietly, "Yes, crazy."

Jason stood, pushing his chair back so hard, it fell over.

"Jason, sit down. Let's talk. Please. I can prove to you I'm telling the truth. I have documents you must see . . . I don't want you to be . . ."

"Shove your documents! I don't want to see your phony documents."

Roy stood up now too and took Jason's arm. Jason broke loose. He spun around. He felt out of control, shaky.

"Your story's bull," he shouted. "I am not your brother! It's impossible! Only a lunatic would make up this twisted twin story!"

Jason stopped and tried to get himself under control. He roughly wiped away his tears, as if he were fighting with them too. His heart cold with hurt, he turned and moved toward the front door.

"Jason, *please*—Jason, come back!" Roy followed Jason and reached out for him, but Jason roughly pushed him away.

CHAPTER 13

August 15, 2026
Massachusetts Institute of Technology
Cambridge, Massachusetts

"Hey, Jason." Jason's dorm mate entered their room and threw his backpack on the floor.

"Hey, Noah."

Sprawled on his bed, Jason looked up from his book. Noah stood tall in their cramped dorm room, grinning. Jason wondered how anyone could always look happy,

"How's it going?"

"Good," Jason replied automatically as he pretty much always did with the other students.

"Well," Noah said as he hurriedly stashed his clothes and books into a duffel bag,"just reminding you I'm going straight to my cousin's and won't be back 'til next month."

"Yeah, I remember," Jason said, though, in fact, he'd forgotten.

"Well, man, don't work too hard," Noah said with a grin as he combed his slick brown hair in the wall mirror.

"Yeah," said Jason.

Noah zipped up the duffel and was out the door.

Jason looked down at his book. He was glad Noah would be gone for three solid weeks. He'd finally get a good chunk of the solitude he'd craved since coming to MIT. He had already gotten a lot of interest and attention from his professors for his hypothesis on random phase approximation, so with Noah at his cousin's house all week, Jason would have the evenings to himself to refine it. Perfect.

He opened his new textbook on augmented reality. After a few minutes, he heard the tiny xylophone sound of a text coming in. He reached under his pillow for his phone.

Not there.

He rifled through the piles of papers and books on his desk.

Nothing.

He looked under the bed where all the stuff lay that he couldn't deal with now—the surprising letter from Melanie, a real letter sent in the mail, the package of socks and stuff from the Kramers and that big-ass envelope, unopened and probably full of bull crap Roy had sent him weeks, maybe months ago, and old homework papers and dirty clothes. He pulled out the clothes, and under a sweatshirt, he felt his phone, drew it out and read:

R u around tonite?

Jason looked at the unknown number. Who could it be?

It wasn't Noah, and he scanned his mind to remember who else might have his phone number.

Jason texted back.

No.

OK. Can I see you 2moro?

Jason stared at his phone screen until jolted by another text coming in.

Ru there?

Yes

So?

OK

OK what. I'm here at MIT now too.

Melanie!

Melanie! Jason looked at the screen in disbelief. He stared at the text for several moments, as if by staring, he'd confirm it was real. He was tempted to text that he had to study and was too busy to see her, but he wanted to see her, *really* wanted to see her, so impulsively he texted:

2moro meet me at Dougie's @ 7

As usual on a Saturday night, Dougie's was crowded. Undergrads and grads mingled in the brightly lit diner, where the smells of fried chicken, hamburgers, hot dogs, fries and chili mingled in one hungry-making aroma.

Jason waited inside near the door, and each time it opened, he cleared his throat and ran his hand over his hair. But the only things entering were cold air and strangers. He looked at his watch. Six past seven. He glanced at the door again, then away. He shouldn't be looking toward the door. That would seem too eager.

He looked around the room. Students were laughing, talking loudly, some of them watching a football game on the big screen above the counter and whooping now and then. As the minutes passed, he wondered why in the world he was meeting her in the first place? She'd probably texted him simply because he was the only one she knew who was also at MIT. That's all. She was probably a bit lonely now and just wanted to meet him for old time's sake.

"Sorry I'm late."

There she was, right in front of him. Her blue denim jacket made her eyes bluer than he thought possible.

"Hi, Melanie."

She hugged him and she smelled beautiful, like peaches. In his embarrassment, he mumbled, "Hungry?"

"Starving," she laughed. "I didn't have lunch today. Been so busy setting up my space in the dorm. I'm in McCormick Hall."

"I'm in Baker House Dorm."

"I know that. I sent you some letters there. Remember? You didn't answer them though. How come?"

"Two?" the hostess asked.

"Yes," Jason said, grateful for the interruption.

Once they were seated in a booth and handed their menus, Melanie said, "You know, I wrote you letters because I didn't have your new email address or your phone number. Finally, I got your phone number from the Kramers. And the Kramers told me they hadn't heard from you either! They were concerned and seemed kind of sad too. Anyway, they knew which dorm you were in, so I just wrote you there. I guess I thought that seeing old-fashioned paper letters would get your attention and you might write back."

"Makes sense," Jason said softly.

"So, didn't you want to write me back?"

A waitress interrupted. "Know what you want?" She stood over them, pen in hand.

After giving their orders, Jason said, "Look, Melanie, I like you. I do. It's just that . . . well, sometimes . . . I don't look at letters much and . . . I mean . . . I read yours . . . but didn't know what to answer."

"Well, you did answer. You sent me an MIT tee shirt. But there was no letter with it. No note attached. No contact information."

"I mean, I didn't know what to *say*."

"Didn't know what to *say*?"

"*How* to say things. I'm not good at . . ." Jason paused. All his feelings for her, all the things he truly wanted to say were blocked inside him and he sat as if paralyzed, unable to say anything.

"You know what? I like the shirt and it fits me and I like hanging out with you, Jason. You're different. You're *interesting*."

He looked at her and smiled. She liked the tee shirt and she thought he was interesting!

Melanie reached across the table and touched his hand. "You know what else? You don't have to explain anything to me right now. Another time."

Jason, who had been looking hard at the glass salt and pepper shakers, now looked up at her.

"So have you heard from the Kramers?" she asked.

"Yeah, they write and send stuff, you know . . . food, gift cards, books."

"Nice."

"Well, they shouldn't. I'm not their foster kid anymore."

"Hear from any of the Clearview kids?" she asked.

"No. I don't."

"Well, I heard something about Matthew."

"Matthew?"

"Yes, Matthew Swundle. He got caught stealing a candy bar."

"A candy bar!" Jason exclaimed. "That's stupid."

"Yes," Melanie said. "Now he's in real trouble. It's on his record."

"For a candy bar!" Jason exclaimed.

"Well, it was the fourth time he'd done it."

"Man, that's dumb," Jason said, looking at her all the while.

Her nails were painted blue like her eyes, and tonight, her hair seemed as shiny as patent leather.

Wow! he thought. *Melanie is the nicest, the smartest and the best-looking girl.*

Melanie slowly wound a strand of hair around her finger as she said, "You know those Mr. Malbrecht holograms you made when we were juniors were awesome. We'd never seen anything like that before; they were so funny!"

"I didn't mean them to be that funny. I've learned a lot since then, how to control a hologram better and, you know, make them way more lifelike. I want to make a hologram so real that you think it's a person. A real person."

"You will," Melanie said confidently. "You sure have the math smarts. I remember those incredible equations you came up with for that project."

"And I remember *your* science project on ignition systems."

"But you arrived late and didn't hear it!"

"I read your report, remember? I liked it. Really did. And I learned from it."

"It was fun to work on, and besides," she laughed, "if I ever lose my key, I could hotwire my own car!"

"Yeah," he said, smiling back at her, feeling something change within him, like a kind of melting.

They lingered over their meal, getting refills of soda just to stay longer. Jason was enjoying the time. She listened to his vision for holography, even the futuristic physics parts and asked smart questions. He listened to her speak passionately about how, one day, electricity would be completely powered from space by some kind of device put there to capture the sun's energy, then transfer it to Earth.

Even when he didn't understand everything she was telling him, he loved her enthusiasm and her intelligence. With Melanie, he felt good. Different than he usually felt. With Melanie, he felt normal.

When the bill came, Jason paid it, then they walked out of Dougie's and toward the campus.

The night was starlit. They walked slowly. Jason wanted to take her hand but felt too shy.

Suddenly Melanie said, "Did you know much about your parents?"

The question took Jason aback. No one had ever asked him this.

"I don't know who my parents were," he said slowly. "No one ever told me. No one ever knew. My last name, Atwood, is just the name Social Services gave me when I was a baby. They made it up. I don't use it, except when I have to."

"Usually *someone* knows your real name," Melanie said. "Someone else in your family, maybe?"

"I don't have any family. No one, so no one knows. I asked my social workers a couple of times to research it for me, but they just said the information doesn't exist. Maybe got lost somehow."

Melanie was quiet and Jason could tell she was thinking about it.

Please don't ask any more questions, he thought.

But when she spoke again, it wasn't a question; it was a statement, and she declared it with a strength that surprised him. "I read once that the Buddha said nothing is ever lost in the universe."

"I don't know what that means," Jason replied. "I mean, I know when old solar systems disintegrate, they're not lost; they turn into cosmic rays."

"I don't really know what it means either," she said. "But it could be," she offered, "that fragments of information about your parents . . . are *somewhere* in our world that are not lost at all, and one day, you'll find them and put those fragments together."

Jason stared at Melanie, astonished. At that moment, it seemed to him not only that she and he thought alike, but that Melanie *knew* him. So, as they strolled together on this glass-clear night, he knew he could love her.

"I know it sounds weird," Melanie continued, "but I

believe you will find who your parents are. Someday, someone or *something* will tell you."

"Maybe," Jason said, unconvinced and feeling way too emotional to say anything more.

They walked onto the campus in silence and soon spoke of other things.

When they reached McCormick Hall, they stopped again and looked at each other.

Melanie was smiling. "I had a good time tonight. I like being with you."

Jason didn't reply, for all he could think of was how much he wanted to gently pull her toward him and kiss her. He imagined her lips, soft and yielding, and how they would hold on to each other with a new yearning.

"Good night, Jason."

Startled out of his reverie, he looked at Melanie's smiling face.

"Good night, Melanie," Jason mumbled, then he watched her walk away.

He didn't want to return to the dorm, so he just kept walking. He felt good—like the outdoors was his own room. The air was warm and the sky seemed but a low ceiling of lights.

He walked aimlessly through the campus, passing boisterous students coming back from parties. As he walked, he thought. He knew he should have kissed Melanie!

After all, didn't she say she *liked* hanging out with him? Didn't she say he was *interesting*? Well, he should have at least taken her hand! But that same old fear had prevented him.

As Jason walked, he savored the memory of being with her. He conjured up her bright smile, her kind words, her intelligent talk, and the good smell of whatever fragrance she wore. Yet soon his thoughts returned to her odd words.

Why would Melanie, a rational, educated girl, believe so strongly that the universe would provide him with information about his family? And how did she seem to know his own deep longing for just that? She had used the words "fragments of information." *Fragments.* Jason tried to remember Crazy Old Roy's rambling.

"Didn't he say something about helping me '*piece*

together the fragments?"

Jason turned and headed back toward his dorm, hurrying past crowds of raucous students. When he reached his room, he yanked off his jacket, knelt on the floor, and stretched his arm out to reach far under the bed. He pulled out the big, sealed envelope Roy had sent him.

Jason sat on his bed, calmed his breath. Then he opened it.

CHAPTER 14

INSIDE THE ENVELOPE, HE FOUND:

1. A letter from Dr. Calvert to Roy explaining his birth situation.

2. The contract between Dr. Ernst Fritzhauer and his parents stating that the embryos were the property of their temporary guardian, Dr. Fritzhauer, for no more than two years, when the guardianship would revert back to Herbert and Lily Anne Kimble.

3. The 1950 Letter of Agreement to transfer one embryo at no cost from Dr. Fritzhauer to Dr. and Mrs. Burt Calvert.

4. The 2008 signed agreement between Rachel Bennington and Dr. Burt Calvert for the

implantation of the second Kimble embryo.

5. The confidential letter of agreement to transfer an embryo from Dr. Fritzhauer to Dr. Calvert.

6. The 2009 DNA test results done with Jason's birth documents, which confirmed the identical twin status of Rachel Bennington's infant and Roy Calvert.

7. The Nevada Child and Family Services papers stating power of jurisdiction over the two-day-old infant boy of unknown parentage, born May 22, 2009.

Jason quickly read the documents. He knew it was true—Roy was his identical twin, but it felt like a cruel trick. Sure, now at last he knew his family, but a family made from abnormal events. And yes, now he had a brother, but his brother was elderly. A senior citizen. An old man!

He lay on his bed and closed his eyes, as if he could shut out all he had just learned. When he opened them again, he saw on the floor in a slim shaft of moonlight a pale blue envelope that had fallen out of the package.

He picked it up and it felt as light as a butterfly. On the outside of the envelope, Roy had written: "Something to her sister—only thing from her left to us." It was a letter his mother had written to a woman in England. The letter had a stamp on it, but the stamp was not postmarked.

To: *Miss Violet Williams*
14 Cobble Lane
Devon
Shropshire
England
United Kingdom

His mother had written those words. *His mother.* He felt the letter's fragile thinness. As thin as his connection to her. He smelled the aged paper, fragrant with loss.

Jason pulled out the brittle, folded sheets—six of them. He looked across at the wall, took a breath, then looked back down at the pages, steeling himself to read them. He took another deep breath. At the top of the letter was written: *Please, Violet, keep private, as you must.*

Jason began to read.

Something was wrong.

It was not a letter.

He looked at each of the pages. No. It was not a letter. The numbered pages held no more than handwritten musical notes. It was some composition, a song or something his mother had written down and sent to his aunt.

No more than that.

In high school, Jason had to take trumpet for two semesters, so he knew how to read music. But this music was complicated, with so many notes and flats and sharps scribbled all over. The song didn't have a name. But what did he care whether it had a name! He'd hoped for a letter, from which he could sense the mind and spirit of his mother.

"Another crap trick!" Jason cried aloud, crumpling the pages into a ball and throwing it across the room, where it fell like a broken dream. Now, more than anything, he wished he hadn't opened that envelope. It was all too weird. Unsettling information about a geriatric twin and a letter that was just a dumb song.

That night, Jason couldn't sleep. He tossed and turned, not able to shut off his smoldering questions. Why would anyone want to keep a song confidential? A *song.* If she had composed it, couldn't she have just copyrighted it? And if she hadn't composed it, what was the point of making it secret? Was his mother as crazy as Roy?

Just before dawn, Jason fell into a restless sleep. He dreamed of being chased by something frightening, yet with no appearance and no name. Then in his dream, he suddenly saw what was chasing him—musical notes! They were flying after him like black birds, dipping and diving right behind him, calling out words! Words he couldn't understand. What were they saying? *What? What?*

Jason woke, his heart beating fast. It was almost noon. He lay in bed with his eyes closed. When his heart calmed, he walked over to the crumpled ball of letters on the floor, smoothed the pages and put them in order.

A.B.C.D.E.F.G. He knew those were the names of the musical notes. Could the song be a code of some kind? What if each note stood for a letter of the alphabet? But there were no musical notes beyond the letter G, so what could she have done for the rest of the alphabet? She would have run out of notes and would have had to create her own code from just those seven notes, perhaps by their repetition or their order or the number of them or the insertion of flats and sharps. Maybe this was some made-up code that only she and her sister knew? If that were true, could he decipher it? If so, perhaps he could unlock yet another secret.

Jason texted Melanie, telling her he was deep into studying and he'd catch up with her as soon as he could.

That week, Jason juggled his schoolwork with researching codes on the internet and at the university's library. Working often until the morning, he tried idea after idea after idea, and when they didn't work, he tried yet another. Researching and trying out codes feverishly, he knew only that whatever he was doing felt like saving his mother *and* saving himself. Then, when three weeks later, fatigued and feverish, he cracked the code and could at last read the letter, his body trembled. For though written a half century ago, his mother's message required action. *Now.*

CHAPTER 15

September 4, 2026

EXHAUSTED AFTER THE THREE-DAY BUS RIDE FROM Massachusetts to Nevada, Jason rang Roy's doorbell.

Roy opened the door. "Well?"

"Well, what?"

"Well, why are you here?"

"I need to talk to you."

"So? You could have called—you didn't have to come thousands of miles."

"It's important."

Jason felt Roy's eyes look him up and down, from his sweat-stained shirt to his dirty tennis shoes.

"Are you going to let me in?"

Roy opened the door wider. Jason walked in, dropped his duffel bag on the rug and collapsed on the sofa. "I read the stuff you sent."

"Finally! You a slow reader or did you have to get your courage up first?"

Jason saw Roy's attitude toward him was different now. Scornful.

Jason knew that, to get through to Roy, he had to let down his guard. But saying what he really felt was new territory for him. Yet, feeling desperate, he gave it a try.

"Look, I know I wasn't fair to you and I'm sorry for what I did . . . everything I did that was bad. I'm sorry. But I've got to tell you something I think you'd want to know. That's why I'm here, so . . ." Jason paused, for he had never asked anyone for anything, and now he hated doing it, but he did. "*Please* listen to me," he said, and his words came out, real. Honest.

Roy made no reply. He walked into the kitchen, came back with a glass of root beer. He handed it to Jason.

"Shoot."

Jason took a gulp, wiped his mouth with the back of his hand and said, "I cracked the code."

"What are you talking about? What code?"

"The code your . . . *our* mother wrote. In the letter that she sent to her sister."

"That was no code. That was some musical composition."

"It was a code."

"How do you know?"

"Because I cracked it."

"This conversation is a circle. Show me what you did."

Jason opened his duffel bag and pulled out a green spiral notebook.

Methodically, he explained to Roy how he'd been curious why their mother would want to keep a piece of music confidential. He did a lot of research and read somewhere that musical notes were at times used as a code. He suspected their mother and her sister had communicated like this for years, maybe starting as kids, doing it for fun. The last three weeks, he'd worked day and night on deciphering the letter, barely sleeping or eating, and by installing a computer program, the kind hackers use, he'd figured it out.

"And?" Roy asked.

Jason handed him the notebook with his translation of his mother's code. Roy picked up his thick brown plastic eyeglasses from the side table, perched them on his nose and began to read.

Jason leaned back against the sofa. He was dead tired. He wanted to sleep. Not talk. Not think.

When Roy had finished reading, Jason heard him softly say, "It's a wonder."

Roy reached into his pocket and pulled out a white handkerchief and wiped his eyes, then his glasses. He folded the handkerchief, put it back in his pocket, looked up at the ceiling, then back down at the letter again.

"She wrote it the day she died," he said softly. Then he began to read it aloud.

"I don't need to hear it," Jason told him. "I've already read it. I'm the one who decoded it, remember? You don't need to read it to me."

Roy continued to read aloud, his voice shaking now:

Dearest Violet,

I am with child. I pray you are sitting down now as you read this for in truth, I am told that I am with children. Triplets! Herbert and I are beyond surprised and over the moon at our thrice blessing.

And now, dear sister, I have some news, even more surprising. I am telling it only to you and only in strict confidence. I beg of you, Violet, do not tell a soul, but rather keep this next news close and closed in your heart.

My doctor has a colleague, Dr. Ernst Fritzhauer, a nice gentleman who has pioneered a way in which I could very safely continue my year-long world concert tour and then bear the triplets a few months after my return. He has kindly offered to remove and freeze the three embryos until then. At first, I was skeptical and even frightened by such an idea as it sounded so curious. But Herbert has convinced me that it is a modern medical solution that will allow me to achieve my career goals before taking on the time-consuming responsibiities of motherhood.

I thank God for this rare opportunity, yet should anything happen to Herbert and me within the next year—should we perish from this Earth, Dr. Fritzhauer has promised to have the embryos 'adopted' with a provision that you are still to be regarded as their aunt. You will forgive me for not designating you as guardian as I wouldn't dream, Violet, of adding a burden (even a joyful one) to your life, given the brave struggle you endure daily with your ill health.

I have also made instructions that, if any or all of them cannot be implanted seventy-five years from our day of return: 10-9-1951, they are to be destroyed.

I weep even as I write this instruction but to keep them alive indefinitely would be yet more unnatural—an affront to Heaven. I selected this timeline. Violet, I cannot bear to think of them destroyed at all. Yet I must provide for all possibilities, no matter how horrid.

God forbid we do not survive our journey, as the aunt to my yet unborn children, you, Violet, must ensure my wishes are carried out. I enclose the address and phone number of Dr. Fritzhauer's clinic in Ithaca, New York.

Your loving sister,
Lily

"*Another* brother," Roy whispered, taking it in. Then, his eyes moistened and his voice raised, cracking with emotion. "Triple wonder! Miracles abound!"

With hands trembling, he put his reading glasses back in their case and shut it with a loud clap.

"Well," he announced, "we need to go."

"Go?" Jason asked. "Go where?"

"Where *he* is, our brother. In Ithaca, New York. Now we know there's a third brother, maybe not even born yet, a twin—I mean, a triplet, maybe looking like us. *Just like us.* We've got to help him. Maybe save him! Jason, we need to go!"

"We don't need to go anywhere. OK, we may have a triplet somewhere, but it's a baby, not a savior. And we're not the wise men. And besides, maybe it's not a baby, maybe it's still an embryo or an old person like you or a ten-year-old or—"

"Whatever he is, he's *ours*," Roy countered. "Family. Our *brother.*"

Jason, rallying beyond his fatigue, said, "I suspected you'd want to do something about it. You're crazy enough to think there's some hope of a seventy-five-year-old embryo being brought to life. But count me out. If there were a third one, they would've done something about it. Your father would've said something about it." He heard his voice rising, felt like he was losing touch with his body. He wanted to leave, to run out of there. "It's insane to think they'd get two born but would leave the other sitting in some freezer."

"Jason—"

"It's stupid, Roy!" He was sick of this, all of it. He finally had a life to live and an actual future, and this man, this . . . brother of his, was messing it up. "Do what you want, but count me out. Anyway, I Googled the Fritzhauer Clinic and nothing came up. No website. Nothing. It's all gone. It's in the past—the past *century*."

"So what? You were born even after you 'sat around in a freezer.' Look, Jason, I don't know why my father didn't say anything about triplets. Maybe he didn't know. Maybe Dr. Fritzhauer didn't tell him there were three for some reason."

"Probably because the third one died," Jason said.

"Maybe. Maybe not. God, don't be so pessimistic, Jason. Don't be so scared. I found you, didn't I? We've got to make sure, one way or the other. Got to learn the truth."

"Why don't we just write the clinic in Ithaca? They don't have a website, but somebody may still be at that address. Let's find out first if we had a brother, *then* go find him. A lot could have happened in so many decades. I still think that embryo was probably destroyed a long time ago."

"Could be," Roy admitted, "but if not, time's running out. If there is a third embryo somewhere, the deadline for its destruction is next month. I want to talk to someone there in person. I want to go to the clinic and see for myself. I'd like to know why I was never told about a third sibling."

"This is a freak thing," Jason argued, "and a long shot I'm not getting involved in." He finally gave in to his desire to flee, making for the door. "I've got important things to do."

"Nothing's more important than this."

"Not to me!" Jason spun, felt anger root him to the spot like a spike driven into the ground. "I don't give a rat's ass! When I had no family and was left with bad people, nobody rescued *me*! So, 'you found me.' Too late! No rescuing needed! I'm not obliged to rescue anybody. Including *you*. And I'm sure not going across the continent to find an unborn someone who probably doesn't even exist. I don't care about an old piece of protoplasm stuck in a freezer!"

"Then," Roy asked, his voice low and steady, "why did you come here? You made quite the journey to give me this information that you now say you don't care about."

"I—" Jason's mind spun around for a reply. Why *did* he rush over? He could've called, or emailed, or texted. "I—I realized I was unfair to you," he sputtered. "I thought you were nuts when you told me we were brothers, but now from the documents, I see this freak fact is true. So I came here to tell you in person, as a matter of information sharing and because I knew that, with the complexity of the code and the deadline looming, it'd be best to explain it all to you in person. That's all. I was being courteous."

"I don't believe you," Roy said.

"Are you saying I'm lying to you?"

"No, I'm saying you're lying to yourself. You didn't sit on a bus for three days to share information or to extend any courtesy."

"Why would I lie to *myself?*" Jason cried. "I've worked my butt off this year to perfect my hologram technology, then I put it all aside, risked my studies, my life, to decipher this ancient letter. I'm scheduled to present an oral term paper in my Honors physics class in a week and a half. I've got to prepare! Even one extra day away will mess me up. I can't sacrifice any more. I can't throw over everything I've worked so hard for to please you!"

"It's not about pleasing me," Roy replied. "There's a deadline to ending the life of our brother. I will never forgive myself if I don't go and at least find out if a viable embryo still exists or if my triplet is walking the earth." Roy's voice cracked with emotion. "Jason, it's not about my wish. It's about our mother's wish. Her last wish is now our destiny. Our mission. And I can't go alone. I'm old."

Jason looked at Roy. He was caught now. Trapped. He knew it was over. He would be giving in to Roy, not because he wanted to, but because he felt that new softhearted feeling he'd felt lately. The feeling he had struggled for so long *not* to feel. Then seeing Melanie, and coming here to Roy...he sensed something cracking open inside him that he didn't want to have crack open. He'd wanted to be strong by staying guarded and distant, yet now he heard himself say: "OK. Shut up about it. *I'll go.* But my scholarship money doesn't cover cross-country trips. I get some money from Social Services each month, but I spent a lot of it on books to learn how to crack codes. I don't have the money this month for airfare, hotels, and food, so you'll have to pay for everything."

"Fine with me. I'll pay. But we won't need airfare and hotels. It's warm. We'll drive."

"Drive! You didn't tell me you wanted to *drive*! It'll take us days to get to New York."

"Five, in fact, and it's the only way to go. We'll see the country. We won't go hunting for, or reserving motels; we'll camp. Won't even need a campground. We'll just pitch a tent anywhere. A lot cheaper, and best of all—we'll see more stars."

"Even one extra day away will mess me up," Jason cried, "but driving could take a week! I can't sacrifice any more. I can't throw over everything I've worked so hard for, just to please you."

"You said that already," Roy replied.

Jason crossed his arms over his chest, his hands fisted. The two stared each other down, similar eyes, one set aged, one young and angry. Jason felt the fire die out. He was so tired. So very, very tired. Roy was exhausting. This situation was exhausting. All he wanted was to sleep. But he had one important thing to tell Roy.

"When I agreed to this, I didn't agree to spend twenty-four hours a day with you in a car and tent. So"—Jason lowered his arms—"you've got to promise that, if at any point, I want to go back, you'll pay my airfare. Promise?"

A smile curled on Roy's lips. "I promise."

CHAPTER 16

ALL AROUND THEM, UTAH'S VALLEY STRETCHED TO THE horizon, the dry, hilly land rolling out like creased paper, as if the land were its own map.

It was only the first day of travel, but even counting the two hitchhikers they'd dropped off, they'd made good time. With his hands lightly on the steering wheel, Roy was singing along to some Italian song on his Dean Martin CD.

From the passenger seat, Jason occasionally looked up from his phone at the landscape. They had driven for five hours so far, yet it looked like they were still in the same place. The endless vista of sagebrush bored him. Even the occasional jack rabbit that would leap across the road looked the same as the last rabbit.

"Can't you play some good music?" Jason asked.

"This *is* good music," Roy said. "Better than your electronic stuff, and besides, you said you didn't want to talk. While I'm driving, you just sit there playing with your phone."

"I'm not playing with the phone; I'm figuring stuff out, programming it. And anyway, I'm used to being quiet and don't see anything wrong with it. If I hadn't lost my earbuds at the last rest stop, I wouldn't have to hear this. I wouldn't have had to listen to you talking your head off to those two hitchhikers you picked up. And I don't understand why you pick up hitchhikers! You're the one who thinks we're on some important mission, so why are we wasting time with strangers?"

"They don't slow us down, and besides, I like meeting people. They're not strangers once you meet them. I like finding out who they are and where they're going and why. Chatting makes the time go faster."

"Time doesn't go faster," Jason replied. "But hitchhikers can be dangerous and—"

"Maybe," acknowledged Roy. "But mostly they're not. They're just people wanting to get some place but don't have the money. It's a kindness to take them."

Jason sighed. "Well, at least don't tell them how

we're related. That'll creep them out. Just say I'm your nephew or your grandson."

"I didn't tell them anything." Roy smiled. "Each time I tried to, you shut me up before I could."

"Well, all I'm saying is, it's nobody's business how we're related, and even if you told them, they wouldn't believe you. And they sure wouldn't believe we're twins! They'd think either you were messing with them or that you're senile."

"Well, maybe I am senile to listen to you spout negativity about good things, like chatting with people, being brothers and . . . Italian songs."

"Speaking of songs," said Jason, returning to his original complaint. "You've been singing the same dumb 1950s songs all day. Don't you have another CD? And why the hell are you using a CD player anyway? They don't even make cars with them anymore."

"That's why I got it installed." Roy grinned before breaking into song again.

"Man, you're annoying." Jason muttered, slumping back in his seat.

They came to a gas station, and while Roy was counting out the cash to pay, Jason saw an older Black man with gray-white hair approaching. The man stood tall.

"Hello, Professor, going far?" he asked in a strong, deep voice.

"As far as New York state," Roy answered.

"That'll do me. I'm heading to Salt Lake City. Much obliged if I could take a ride with you and the young fellow."

"Sure, no problem. We've got room and we aim to reach Wendover before suppertime."

The man smiled. "Sweet!" he said.

Roy opened the rear car door and the man threw his duffel bag on the back seat and slid in beside it.

"I'd sure thank you again, Professor, if I got your name and your grandson's."

"Roy's my name, and the boy here is Jason. He's not my grandson. He's my . . ."

"Nephew," Jason said quickly, "*nephew.*"

"Joyful to meet you both, Mr. Roy and Mr. Jason, and a thank you to you too. My name's Oscar Llewellyn Beaufort."

"Well, we're joyful to meet you too, Mr. Beaufort," Roy sang cheerily. "Aren't we, Jason?"

"Yeah, we are," Jason muttered.

Roy started the engine and Oscar unzipped his duffel bag and drew out a harmonica.

"Mind if I play?"

"Do you know *Volare?*" Roy asked, grinning. Jason swatted his shoulder.

"Who doesn't! If you're talking about that old Italian song Dean Martin used to sing, I can play that to beat the band."

Oscar wiped his mouth with the back of his hand, then cupped both hands around the harmonica as if it were a sandwich. He began to play the song slowly and so soulfully that, against the background hum of the car's air conditioning, there floated a bluesy saxophone sound.

"Wow!" Roy said. "You're good."

Oscar grinned, "Should be by now, been practicing near sixty years."

Oscar continued to play, and Jason began to relax. He liked the man's harmonica playing and it sure beat Roy's singing.

"Are you a musician?" he asked the man.

"No, I'm a pugilist. Well, looky here, I just lied!

Truth is, I *was* a pugilist."

Oscar said the word "pugilist" with such reverence that Jason, not knowing what a pugilist was, thought the man was a kind of preacher.

"You were a boxer?" Roy asked.

"Long time ago, Roy. Long time ago."

"Heavyweight?"

"Yes, sir. Heavyweight. I done 'em all. Some I beat and some beat me. I was never great, but I was good. *Real* good."

"Ever fight Sugar Ray?"

"Yep. Twice. Beat him once."

"That must've felt good," said Roy.

Oscar laughed. "Felt better than a hot shower, tell you that. I was puffed up and famous for nearly a month!" He laughed again with a wheezing sound like a door hinge needing oil.

"What do you do now?" Roy asked.

"Well, I'm old as stone, so I just get about. Going to Salt Lake to visit one of the fellows I fought back in '81. I stay close to all the fellows I fought—the ones still breathing. We're like a family. I call 'em my Punch Pals."

By sunset, they had reached the town of Aragonite.

Roy exited the freeway and parked at the Busy Bee Diner. When the three stepped out of the car, the hot desert air hit them like a fist.

Roy and Jason ordered their tuna sandwiches and root beers and Oscar ordered chicken fried steak and coffee.

When the check came, Roy drew out some bills from his wad of cash and placed them on the check tray.

"Wait a minute, Professor!" Oscar said, plucking the check from Roy's hand. "I can see you're about to pay for me and I won't be supporting that. Put your money away. I'm paying for you and your nephew. I'm thankful for you hauling me."

"You don't need to do that . . ." Roy started but Oscar hushed him.

"Looky here." Oscar jabbed his finger at the check. "You had your mind set on paying this thing without even seeing it. That's not right. Man, you always got to peruse the check! You've got to look out for the feint!"

"The what?" Jason asked.

"The *feint.* F-E-I-N-T. It's a way to distract someone. You see, some folks—they're rascally. They'll shoeshine you into believing things. They might add an extra root beer or something on the check and you're so happy with your belly full, you don't even notice. Yes, folks will do it. And, they don't care if you're old. Shoot! They'd mess with Methuselah!"

Oscar took off his glasses and bent low over the bill to read it. After he had read it, he lay down the cash for it. "Well, this one's clean, but Professor, you be more watchful next time. And you, Jason," Oscar said, looking closely at him. "I sense you're a lot like your uncle—*a lot*—I just feel it somehow. You're two of a kind. Yes, sir, I see that same's your game so, young fellow, you be watchful too."

Out in the parking lot, Jason surprised himself by asking, "Can you teach me a feint?"

"Can I teach you a feint? Can I teach you a feint! Why, I could teach you a hundred, but I'll teach you a beauty right now."

The three walked to the side of the diner's parking lot.

"All right, young feller, come after me swinging!" Oscar called.

Jason, feeling jumpy, stepped forward and punched out his right arm.

"Hey, we're not playing!" Oscar called. "I mean for you to hit me, not dust lint off me. C'mon. Sock it to me!"

Oscar and Jason danced around each other like roosters. When Oscar finally lifted his arm to swing at Jason's right side, Jason didn't flinch. He stood his ground, catching Oscar's left arm, shoving it downward, avoiding the punch that was coming at him.

Oscar grinned, "Oooh, boy! You sure learned that somewhere! Yes, sir! Somehow you *already* learned the first rule of Feint! Get your opponent ready to stop what you're aiming to do, then *don't do it!* Get the sucker ready for the *wrong* thing. Yep, you got it. But, looky here, young Jason, you need to use foot feints too. What do I mean? I mean, you move your feet one way, but you go the other. Watch." Oscar demonstrated how he could move his feet by the smallest increments to the left then, without warning, jump to the right.

When Jason tried it, he found he could do it. He was surprised at his own agility and wondered why he was so good at it.

As Roy watched, chuckling, Oscar beamed at Jason in admiration, then without warning swung at him. Jason ducked, forcing Oscar to punch air.

"Jason, you sure learn fast!" Oscar declared. "Remember what I told you and you'll be sweet."

Jason looked down, smiling in embarrassment.

"But Jason, here's one last bit of intelligence for you. Always watch the guy's *eyes*. And not just when fighting. You can tell a lot by watching the eyes of folks. We used to say, 'For them that's sly, the eyes don't lie.' What does that mean? It means someone may know more tricks than you—with their arms and their feet and their head, but it's *their peepers* that will give you clues to what'll happen next. Always. That's 'cause no one on this here earth can make their eyes lie, so watch them close and you'll trick 'em true."

People now leaving and arriving at the Busy Bee diner had formed a small crowd, watching Jason and Oscar Llewellyn Beaufort.

"Well, that's enough," Oscar said. "You got the point good. Besides, I think folks here seeing me hit a white boy might be inclined to get some peculiar ideas."

They drove into Salt Lake City, dropped Oscar off at his friend's house, then drove for another hour. At nightfall, they turned off Highway 80 onto a dark narrow road at the side of the Wasatch mountains. Here, in a cold valley, they pitched their blue nylon dome tent, far away from the car lights on the road. Roy shunned campgrounds because he said the noise of people talking all around wasn't real camping.

"You might as well as sleep in a shopping mall as sleep in a campground," he had told Jason.

Roy made a small fire and Jason took photos of the rising black smoke and the flames, which in the darkness, grew, danced, and quivered like living things.

"So," Roy suddenly said. "Those holograms you're making . . . why?"

"Why what?"

"Why are you making them? What's the point? Why are you so interested in holograms?"

Jason, looking up at the sky, said, "They're cool. They're a kind of Deepfake? You know what that is?"

"Sure, it's a photoshopped video that looks like the real person is saying and doing things, but it's fake. It can fool people. Dangerous stuff."

"Well, I'm not working on stuff to fool people, but to help them."

"How?"

"I think holograms could be used for image

guidance to operate on people. Doctors could render a 2D image into a 3D hologram of a person to help them plan their treatment better."

"You mean like they could zoom in and out of a hologram, which would be a replica of a person—see all their insides?"

"Yeah, they could plan their surgeries better or use the hologram for teaching doctors—and that's just medicine. I think the military could use holograms too—like make illusions to fool the enemy."

"Impressive. You thought this out. I did read about possible holographic displays of battlefields, but it sounds like what you're doing is something new. But you're using just a phone, so explain the science to an old optics guy like me."

So Jason explained it, and later in their sleeping bags, Jason and Roy talked science for a long while. Jason liked this best. During the day, he and Roy seemed so different, not like twins at all. But now, talking about science, it was as if they thought with one mind. That felt good. He liked learning things from Roy about physics and programming that helped him refine what he now called his Hyper-Hologram technology.

When at last Roy was snoring peacefully, Jason poked his head out of the tent and looked up at the unlimited sky. He felt different. Maybe it was Mr. Beaufort showing him those tricks, but maybe it was more than that. He was starting to see the size of things—a road that stretched across states, the vastness of the desert, and a sky wider than he had ever seen. The great open spaces made him think of mind-boggling ideas—like, what if the universe was a hologram? If a hologram is just a 3D image embedded in a 2D format, maybe what appears as 3D reality is really stored on a 2D surface that includes time. If that were true, would that mean everything he saw was an illusion? He looked up at the sky and felt that he belonged to it somehow. He was beginning to feel as if he were not truly an orphan but had a rightful home in the universe. He felt real.

And with this feeling, the thought of Melanie came to Jason yet again. He thought of her throughout the day and just before he fell asleep each night. Now, he dug out his phone and answered the text she had sent. He wanted to type:

On short trip

Miss you lots

But he typed:

On short trip

TTYL

With the text sent, he snuggled down into his sleeping bag and fell asleep. He woke only once to leave the tent to pee. When he returned, he saw Roy was not in his sleeping bag and had probably gone out to pee too.

But Roy did not return.

Not in five minutes, not in ten, not in twenty.

Jason walked toward the car. No one inside or around it.

"Roy!" he called.

He walked back to the tent

Not there.

"Roy! Roy! Roy! Roy!"

Again and again, Jason yelled out Roy's name at the top of his lungs.

But the only sound that came back was the lone hoot of an owl.

CHAPTER 17

JASON STOOD IN FRONT OF THE TENT, FLOODED WITH anger. It was just like crazy Roy to wander off in a desert and get lost. At night!

And if Roy couldn't hear Jason's yelling, he must have wandered far. *Well, let him wander! I'm not risking freezing to death in a desert for that old coot.* Jason entered the tent, slipped into his sleeping bag and zipped it up. He lay there, but sleep would not come. He sat up.

Damn!

Jason reached for the flashlight, but it wasn't at the left side where they kept it. In the dark, he felt all around the inner sides of the tent and under the sleeping bags.

Nothing.

Damn! He would have to go find Roy in the desert without light.

He put his shoes and parka back on, stuck his hands in the pockets for warmth, and started walking. Even in a desert, he knew directions because he knew how to read the constellations, but what help was that? Since he didn't know where Roy was, it didn't much matter which direction he went. *I'll just walk around a little and call his name,* he thought, then comforted himself with a new thought. *At his age, Roy couldn't have gone far.*

The air felt snow-cold. He walked faster simply to stay warm but soon realized that wasn't possible. His parka wasn't meant for this kind of cold and he shivered. As he went, his mind churned with thoughts. He regretted coming on this trip and thought unhappily of what he was missing at MIT. If he found Roy, he'd tell him that he wanted to go back, and first thing in the morning too. Yes, he'd keep Roy to his promise. *I have things to do,* he told himself, *and this isn't one of them.*

He came to a hill and decided to climb up to get a vantage point, and from higher up, he figured his shouts for Roy would carry farther.

He couldn't see a trail in the blackness, so he started very slowly climbing up the hillside. He couldn't see more than a few feet in front of him. Suddenly, he heard a human sound—like laughter! He froze. The sound was eerie in its repetitiveness, its sameness.

Jason's heart revved like an engine. He climbed faster, stumbled over a rock and flew forward, landing on his stomach, bruising his knees and cutting his right hand. The laughing sound got louder, and as Jason stood up, his hand burning in pain, he sure hoped the sound wasn't human, for if it was, it would be a malevolent one. The sound stopped and started up again, then Jason figured it out. Coyote.

Now his ears were tuned like antennae to the sounds of the desert. He was startled by the screech of a hawk and heard, among the rocks, the nervous scuttling of lizards. He hiked for what felt about an hour to him, calling out as he went, "ROY! ROY, WHERE ARE YOU? ANSWER IF YOU CAN! ROY! ROY!"

Nothing.

Jason's anger turned to fear. *Why didn't Roy hear him?* The only reason that made sense was that Roy *couldn't* hear him. Something bad must have happened to him. *I finally found a family member and now he may be dead,* Jason thought, *and I didn't even get to know him.* Jason's heart was beating hard against his chest. He couldn't tell if it was from the strenuous climbing or the terror he felt that something very bad had happened to Roy.

The moon rose, so now Jason could make out that he was halfway up the hill and he could see all around the hazardous outlines of cacti. He was really cold now. His feet felt numb inside his sneakers and his ears ached from the blade-sharp air. He went on, climbing higher and higher, almost robotically. He breathed in the bitter smells of sagebrush and earth. He kept his bloody hand in his parka pocket and used his other hand to grip rocks as he climbed to steady himself. He went slower than he wanted as he stepped carefully around the cacti. When he finally made it to the top, he saw he was on a flat, table-top hill—a mesa.

He looked around. In the shadowy darkness, he could make out where the cliff edge fell sharply. And, at that far edge, in the ash-gray light of the risen moon, he saw it.

Roy's body, lying face up.

CHAPTER 18

JASON RAN TOWARD THE BODY.

Wearing his down parka and knit hat, Roy lay motionless. His eyes, unblinking, were open as if staring at the sky. Jason knelt and took his hand to feel for the pulse.

"Wanna dance?"

Jason jumped back. "You're alive!"

"Always was."

"What the hell are you doing up here?" Jason cried. "Why did you wander off?"

Roy, still lying on his back, said, "Looking at stars, thinking of things. And I didn't wander off; I went for a walk."

"Who the hell goes for a walk in a desert at night! And alone! You really are insane! You're on top of a cliff that's hard going. That's not a walk!"

"Wrong. There's a nice wide trail that leads up here."

"A trail?" Jason, irate at his wasted effort climbing up through cacti and rocks, sputtered, "Why didn't you tell me you were leaving!"

"I'm sorry I scared you. I didn't mean to. Really. I'm sorry, but you were asleep and I didn't want to wake you up just to tell you I was taking a walk."

Jason looked hard at Roy and the anger within him burst into a firestorm.

"Well, you should have done that! You could have been killed! Attacked by a mountain lion or rattlesnake or, at your age, fallen off a cliff!"

"Not likely," Roy said, sitting up. "I memorized the path, and besides, it's hard to fall off a cliff when you've got a strong flashlight."

Jason saw the flashlight lying beside Roy. The flashlight he himself had looked for and needed. He picked it up and hurled it far over the cliff. "FUCK THE FLASHLIGHT!"

Roy sat up. "What's the matter with you?"

"Nothing's the matter with me. *I'm* sane. Except I

was nuts to come on this trip. I should have known it wouldn't work with someone crazy like you."

"Well, I'm not so crazy to throw our only flashlight off a cliff. Why did you do that?"

"I could've gotten killed looking for you! Now I see all the trouble I took out here freezing my ass, bruising my knees, and cutting my hand was a waste of time. A friggin' waste of time!" Jason shivered again. No, it wasn't shivering. He was trembling now from both the cold and his hot emotions. He felt it so deep, that fire of anger that could be so easily lit and now it was consuming him.

"I don't care about the flashlight!" he cried. "And if you care about it, jump off the cliff and get it. I don't care a damn about it and I don't care a damn about you!"

"Seems you cared enough to come looking for me."

"I DON'T CARE A DAMN ABOUT YOU!" Jason shouted.

"Maybe you don't care a damn about anyone," Roy countered.

"You don't know shit about me."

"I think I do. I think you work awfully hard to not

care about anyone. Yes, that's it."

"Oh, so now you're a shrink?" Jason let out a false laugh.

"You work at not caring and not feeling," Roy went on. "You've been doing it your whole life."

"SHUT UP! WHY WON'T YOU SHUT UP!"

Roy didn't seem afraid of Jason. He stood and walked slowly toward him, speaking to Jason in a low voice.

"I'm not going to shut up because, yes, I know about you. I know why you were so quick to learn Oscar's feints."

"SHUT UP, ROY! SHUT UP WITH YOUR SENILE BLABBER!"

Jason walked away, but Roy followed him. "You were quick to learn the feints because you didn't have to learn them. You already knew them. You already knew those quick steps and when to duck. You learned those feints years ago when you were hit. Yes, you learned early on how to protect yourself from the blows of bad grown-ups. You used feints for years without even knowing you were using them. And as you grew, you also learned to protect yourself from the blows by telling yourself you don't care."

"SHUT UP! ROY, SHUT UP! YOU'RE TALKING CRAZY!" Jason was desperate to get away, but when he spun around to flee, he got disoriented and, in the bitter-cold night, he was trembling worse than ever. He felt sick, like he needed to throw up.

Roy showed no mercy. He followed Jason, caught up with him, grabbed his arm. "You'll do anything to ward off hurt by covering it over with indifference or anger. But you hurt. Jason, you *hurt.*"

No one had ever talked to him like this. No one had ever *known* him like this. It was as if somehow Roy could read his mind. No, not his mind—his *soul.* The truth of Roy's words made the thing Jason had sealed up within him his whole life now start to crack again. This time, he couldn't stop the cracking. He felt as if a glacier were breaking inside him.

His eyes were so filled with tears, he could hardly see and he was shaking now. Shaking bad. His teeth rattled like a skeleton. He tried to get away, but wherever he turned, Roy blocked him. Finally, he pushed Roy out of the way so hard, Roy fell.

Roy was unhurt. Slowly, he got up and stood his

ground. He didn't approach Jason this time, but he kept his eyes on him, whispering, "And yet, you came looking for me . . . in the dark and in the cold. So, *who* are you?"

Jason couldn't answer. Couldn't talk. He wanted to yell at Roy again, but within him, the glacier was shattering so violently, he felt his body was being taken over by a force over which he had no control.

"*Who* are you?" Roy whispered again, and when Jason didn't answer, he whispered it again even softer, "*Who* are you?"

With an animal cry of pain, Jason collapsed on the ground. Hunched over, he sat with his head buried in his arms and wept. Jason's shoulders heaved up and down as his sobs came in piercing wails. He cried so hard it was like vomiting, as if his sobs were purging his deepest pain. Roy sat beside him for a long while. When Jason's sobs slowed, then finally stopped, and his breathing again felt normal, Jason looked up at the sky. Roy looked up too and neither one uttered a word.

Then Roy said, "Stars are funny things. They're like brothers. You could call them *Star Brothers*. They look like they're alone—like single sparks of light, but they're not. Almost all stars are born in pairs. Twins. Or triplets. It's *together* they give off light."

Roy stood up, then Jason stood up. In the dim moonlight, they helped each other back to the tent. Roy used his handkerchief to bind Jason's bleeding hand and his memory of the trail allowed them to return quickly. At times, though shivering himself, Jason held Roy's elbow to steady him as they carefully made their way downward in the darkness.

That's how they went. Helping each other. Brothers.

CHAPTER 19

IN WYOMING, THE HIGHWAY SHOT AHEAD ARROW-straight. The sagebrush of the plains lay on the ground, gray as fog, and far in the distance, the snow-capped mountains loomed skyward like a promise.

"She was different, wasn't she?" Jason said.

"She was different," Roy agreed. "I think our mother cared deeply about whatever she did, about her music and her marriage . . ."

"And about us," Jason said.

"Yes, about *us*. She wrote that letter because she wanted to make sure we were safe and cared for. More than that—she wanted to save us. And I believe she wrote it in code to protect our privacy. In those days, her decision to freeze her embryos would have been shocking to most people. She must have trusted her sister immensely." Roy gripped the steering wheel harder as he said, "Yet we'll never know why she didn't send the letter. If she had sent it, what happened may not have happened."

"You mean our being born so many years apart?"

"Yes and our triplet . . . he would have been born along with us. Now we don't even know if he'll ever be born."

"Maybe was already born."

"Maybe," Roy acknowledged, then added, "She tried, Jason. Our mother tried to care for us. She loved us. That letter you figured out proves it. We can take comfort now, knowing for certain she loved us."

"She loved us before we were even born," Jason said, and the thought astonished him and made him yearn for his mother.

Yet he was yearning for a ghost—someone who died nearly sixty years before he was born. She died knowing neither him nor Roy, and they would both die never knowing her. And he would never know his almost-mother, Rachel Bennington. Would Rachel have loved him, and he loved her? Jason sat thinking, overwhelmed with emotion, frightened to at last let emotion take him over . . . but, for the first time in his life, willing.

After a while, his mind returned to Melanie. Next time he saw her, he would take her dancing somewhere. She'd once told him she liked dancing. Yes, even though he didn't know how to dance, he would take her. And next time he saw her, he would kiss her. No doubt about that. He would kiss her, for sure. And something else too, he'd do. He'd tell her how much he liked her. Maybe he'd even tell her what he really felt. That he loved her because now he could tell *himself* that, and it felt good.

After crossing into Nebraska and passing North Platte around noon, they spotted a young man by the side of the road. He was tall and slim, and he wore a black sport jacket, gray jeans, and white shirt. A black messenger bag was slung over his shoulder. With one hand, the man held the handle of his small, brown, wheeled suitcase and with the other, he held his thumb out.

"Roll down the window," Roy told Jason as he slowed the car to a stop. Jason sighed and rolled down the passenger window as Roy, leaning over the steering wheel, called, "Where are you heading?"

"Omaha."

"Then, you're invited."

"Much obliged, sir."

"My name's Roy and this here is my . . . this is Jason."

"Pleased to meet you. My name is Ian Withers."

"Nice meeting you, Mr. Withers," Roy said cheerily. "I can tell from your accent you flew across the pond."

"Yes, I'm from Manchester, England."

Roy steered back onto the highway and, as Jason knew he would, Roy got talkative.

"What's in Omaha? Must be something special, dressed the way you are."

"Indeed. An astrology conference. I'm quite eager to get there as I missed the bus in North Platte and didn't fancy waiting four hours for the next one."

"An astrologer!" Roy exclaimed. "I like looking at stars myself, and so does Jason."

Jason silently groaned.

"Of course," Roy added with a grin, "I don't believe in astrology. I'm a Scorpio, and we're skeptical."

The young man sighed as if he had heard this joke many times. "There are lots of people who think astrology is rubbish," he said, "but they simply are ill-informed. They think we astrologers are off our trolley, but astrology has endured for thousands of years, so perhaps we're not."

"I didn't mean to offend you, Ian," Roy said.

"No offense taken, sir," the young man replied as he took out some papers from his messenger bag.

Roy let the man read his papers undisturbed, making Jason grateful for Roy's good sense in knowing when *not* to talk.

About an hour and a half later, Roy pulled into a rest stop. They had bought a jug of orange juice in town and the three sat outside the restrooms on benches around a stone table. In the hot dry air, they sipped the cold juice with pleasure. Ian reached into his messenger bag and drew out six wrapped cheddar cheese and lettuce sandwiches on white bread. He handed two each to Roy and Jason.

"We can't eat your food," Roy protested.

"I made a good lot—too many really—in case I got hungry on the bus," Ian replied, "but really, I don't need them all and am happy to share them. Please. Enjoy."

"Thank you," Jason mumbled. He was hungry, and

when he bit into the sandwich, the sharp cheese with the somewhat wilted lettuce tasted delicious to him.

"You two," Ian started, "are rather different."

"Different?" Jason asked.

"What I mean is that you are different in that you seem so alike—*quite* alike really. Grandfather and grandson?"

"Not exactly," Roy said, "but we are alike—*rather* alike."

"Maybe you could read our signs," Jason said to change the subject. "If that's OK with you."

"Absolutely. Not a bother at all. I can do a quick one." Ian swallowed his last bite of sandwich, and from his bag, drew out some charts, a notebook, and a calculator.

"Let's start with you, Mr. Roy. What is your date of birth?"

"November 4, 1951."

"All right, 4 November, 1951—Yes, it's all coming clear. Yes, indeed, you are a Scorpio." Ian unfolded a multi-colored chart until it was as large as a placemat. The chart was packed with planets, stars, circles, and lines.

Mumbling to himself while making his long fingers fly over the calculator, he jotted down notes in the little book, and after a few minutes, said, "Well, I think what I'm about to say, you pretty much know.

"You are brave, stubborn, a true friend, and I daresay, Mr. Roy, you like to reveal secrets, to learn the truth. You hate dishonesty and are brave. And you understand well the rules of the universe."

Roy chuckled. "Very good, Ian. Very good and very true. I'm starting to warm to this astrology stuff."

Ian smiled, showing straight, even teeth in a pleasant, kindly face that was as pale as a peeled potato. He turned to Jason, "Now you. May I have your date of birth please?"

"May 22, 2009."

"22 May, 2009—All right, let's see what kind of bloke you are."

Ian looked at Jason "Yes, you are a Gemini. Would have guessed it, really. Yes, you are certainly twins."

Startled, Roy and Jason froze.

Ian grinned, "Oh, don't look so frightened! I wasn't being literal, of course. Obviously, you couldn't really be twins! I mean, Gemini is the constellation of the twins, Castor and Pollux. Gemini is *the sign* of twins, *that's* what I mean."

"Of course," Roy said with a weak laugh as Jason sat quiet.

"Now, Jason, do you happen to know the time you were born?"

"No," Jason replied.

"No worries," Ian replied. "If I can't work with a sun sign or the time of birth, I look as well at the fixed stars around your constellation, the asteroids and the minor planets." Ian bent to his work, poring over the colorful chart and alternately taking notes and rapidly tapping the calculator. When he finally looked up again, he said, "Jason, as a Gemini, you are curious, most likely interested in science and have a love of family. Truth is a guiding force in your life as well. You have a deep emotional side I suspect you don't reveal, and you like time by yourself to think and create. As a Gemini 'twin,' you may have quite a different emotional life within than what you show to the world. That's the duality, the *twin-ness* of Gemini."

"Hmmm," was all Jason said.

Ian took a sip of juice, then suddenly looked back

down at his chart. After several moments, his brow furrowed. He squinted hard over his notes, then pulled out his laptop, and on some program, entered what seemed to Roy and Jason like a lot of information. Finally, he stopped, looked up, perplexed, and muttered, "Most peculiar."

"What's wrong?" Jason asked.

"Nothing wrong, but I daresay, unusual. Most unusual. Peculiar, even."

"What's peculiar?" Roy asked impatiently.

"It's that you, Jason, though born under a completely different sign, and even when I incorporated the possible star signs, your cusp, the appropriate asteroids, planets, and stars . . . well, you have a most similar, dare I say, nearly identical horoscope to Mr. Roy."

"You mean in terms of our personalities?" Jason asked. "We're really not alike."

"I beg to differ," Ian said. "Your personalities may *appear* somewhat different but that's the gloss of it, so to speak. In fact, you each seem to have implausibly similar interests, temperaments, likes, dislikes, tendencies, and emotions. You're alike as socks. Most peculiar."

Jason said nothing as he and Roy received this information, for he felt that it was not only uncanny, but eerie.

"Yes, peculiar!" Roy agreed with a little too much surprise in his voice. "Well, thank you very much, Ian. Jason and I appreciate this new knowledge, but we better be off now."

Ian had looked a bit numbed by his discovery but now perked up, saying cheerily, "Before we go, I must say that I see that both your lives will be rather interesting from what I saw in the heavens. Mind you, astrology can never be completely accurate. I'm not a fortune-teller, but I feel some sort of important undertaking is beckoning each of you. Oh, I know this may sound rather grand, but that is what I see in the charts."

Jason and Roy merely looked at him as they took in this information.

Ian continued, "And yet I presume, because of your temperaments and unique qualities that your lives should be tickety-boo."

"Tickety-boo?" Jason and Roy asked in unison.

"Yes, tickety-boo, you know, just fine, all right, or as you Yanks would say, OK."

By early evening, they had dropped Ian off at the Omaha Convention Center, then drove toward Cunningham Lake to find a place to set up their tent. Jason felt good, even happy.

Roy too was feeling good, for suddenly he laughed and shouted, "THE REST OF OUR LIVES ARE TICKETY-BOO! *TICKETY, TICKETY, TICKETY, TICKETY-BOO!*"

Jason laughed and said the new word over and over too, until the silliness of the sound overwhelmed him and he yelled, "*TICKETY-BOO! HAPPY HALLOWEEN!*"

"TICKETY-BOO AND TYLER TOO!" Roy whooped.

"*TICKETY-BOO—AND I'LL STICK IT TO YOU!*" Jason cried in a mock English accent.

"*YOU'RE PERFIDIOIUS WHEN FASTIDIOUS!*" hooted Roy.

"*TICKETY-BOO TO PERSNICKETY YOU!*"

They were gleeful when Jason suddenly cried, "Wait! I just thought of something!"

"Go on, as long as it's . . . *tickety-boo!*" chuckled Roy.

"No, listen, it's important. Stop the car!"

Roy pulled to the side of the road as Jason's voice had turned serious.

"Remember what Ian said when you told him your birthday?"

"Well, I know he wrote it down."

"Yes, but before he did that, he repeated the date aloud. You told him November 4, 1951. But he said '4 November 1951.' I told him May 22nd, 2009 and he said '22 May 2009.'"

Roy said, "So? That's what they do across the pond and in most places in the world—they put the day before the month. What's the big deal?"

"The big deal is that our mother was English and the deadline she noted in the letter may not be what we think!"

"Let's look at it again," Roy said calmly.

Jason got out and opened the trunk. He drew out the envelope with the documents and came back to the front seat with their mother's letter.

By the interior car light, they read the date their

mother had put on the letter itself:

7-11-1950.

"The plane went down on November eighth," Roy said, "and she had only just learned she was pregnant, so the number seven couldn't be July, as that would have been five months earlier! No, it's not the seventh month; it's the seventh *day* of the eleventh month, November. The date of this letter is November seventh."

"*Agggggghhhh!*" cried Jason. "*We* should have seen that! Now let's look at the deadline."

10-9-2026

Roy said, "It's not October ninth?"

"No, it's September tenth!" Jason cried. "*Today is September seventh. We only have two days!*"

Roy and Jason read the panic on each other's faces.

"We better keep going," Roy said, starting the engine. "From here, Ithaca's almost a thousand miles away. I don't see sleep in our horoscope."

CHAPTER 20

They roared through Iowa and were cruising through Illinois when Jason asked,

"How come you haven't let me drive?"

"Maybe I'm fussy about who drives my car."

"What's so special about your car?"

"It's mine, that's what."

"Well, you've been driving for six hours straight, which you said was your limit. And you've been yawning like a hippo, so let me drive. We've got to keep going."

Roy gripped the steering wheel harder as he said, "Do you even know how to drive a stick shift?"

"I can drive anything: stick shift car, motorcycle, truck . . . Well, maybe not a really big truck."

"When did you learn to drive a motorcycle?"

"From a science report."

"You're joking."

"No, really. I have a friend, Melanie, and in high school, I read her report on ignition systems and that got me interested in them. So, I watched some YouTube videos on vehicles—how you start up a motorcycle and drive it and how their engines work—how they rev a lot higher than a car's and have a greater power to capacity ratio. I rode one too—twice."

"Impressive," Roy laughed. "You must have really liked that girl."

"She's nice."

"Well, she must be, from the way you're blushing. OK. You can drive but remember, watch the speed limit—we can't afford to get stopped by the police. And don't grind the gears. I can't stand when people grind the gears. And show me your license."

Roy pulled off the road. Jason dug in his pocket for his wallet and showed Roy his license, saying, "I never used it because I never owned a car, but I can drive."

Roy handed him the key and Jason slid into the driver's seat. He turned the key in the ignition, and with a shudder, shot off.

"Don't grind the gears!" Roy growled, then, as the sun faded from the sky, he fell asleep.

By midnight, they had crossed most of Iowa. Roy woke and drove again while Jason sat in the backseat and looked for a text from Melanie. There was none, even though he had sent her three in the last couple of days. He hadn't told her anything really, nothing about what he was doing, just asking about her. He turned off his phone, closed his eyes and soon was asleep. When he woke, it was morning and they were somewhere past a town called Newton. Here, everything in the countryside had a yellow tinge to it—the drying corn fields, the hay bales, the golden butterweed at the crop edges, and the pale ceiling of sky washed yellow by sunlight.

"Breakfast time!" Roy announced as he drove into the parking lot of the Over Easy Diner.

"We can't stop for breakfast," Jason said. "We don't have time. We can stop only to use the restroom."

"We've got to eat," Roy replied.

"Look, you were the one who said, 'we won't have time to stop.' Didn't you say that?"

Roy didn't answer.

"And you were the one who said, 'There's a deadline to saving our brother,' and you'd never forgive yourself if you didn't find out if he exists at all."

"We'll eat fast," Roy said. "We can't just keep driving without even a quick break to eat and stretch our legs. We're human, aren't we?"

Jason saw Roy's bloodshot eyes and how his cheeks had a hollowed look, as if his face had become deflated like a worn tire. It hit him again—Roy was elderly. Roy was *old*.

Jason sighed. "OK, let's eat."

The Over Easy diner was small, but Roy said it was the way he liked diners. Small with vinyl booths, '50s chrome jukeboxes on the tables, the smell of bacon frying and waitresses past middle age wearing uniforms.

As soon as they sat down, one of the waitresses, a buxom woman with red lipstick thick as candle wax and hair the color of potato chips, handed them the plastic menus.

"Good morning, boys," she sang cheerfully. "My name's Lillian and I'm going to take darn good care of you. How about starting off with some coffee to wake you up good?"

"That's the ticket," Roy said.

She poured coffee into Roy's mug, then turned to Jason. "What about you, cutie, want coffee?"

"Sure," Jason mumbled, not looking at her.

"Well, your grandson's shy. Does he take after you?"

"He's his own man," Roy said.

The waitress winked. "Sweetheart, I bet you're your own man too . . . or some lucky woman's."

"We know what we want to eat," Jason told her, handing back the menus.

"Sure, what can I get you?"

"The Denver omelet, a side of bacon, and the buckwheat pancakes."

"Denver omelet, bacon, buckwheat pancakes," she repeated, smiling at Jason.

"You got it."

She turned back to Roy and placed her hand lightly on his shoulder, "What about you, sweetheart?"

"I'll have the same."

"Well, aren't you two peas in a pod!" She laughed then added, "Your orders are coming right up."

"She's annoying," Jason said when the waitress left.

"She's just doing her thing," Roy replied.

Jason watched her walk away. She paused to laugh with a man at the next table, and playfully swatted him with the menu.

Returning with their orders, the waitress leaned far over the table to set down the plates, so that her substantial bust hovered before them.

"The cook," she whispered, "he puts two pancakes on a plate, but I said to him, 'Those fellows look hungry enough to eat a horse and chase the jockey, so better put three.'" She winked at Roy again.

"Thank you, ma'am," Roy said. "It's appreciated."

"You can call me Lillian. Friendlier than *ma'am*. And what can I call *you*?"

Roy grinned at her, "Call me anything, just don't call me late for dinner."

Lillian laughed too long at his joke and only stopped when he said, "My name's Roy and this is Jason."

"Well, I'm pleased to meet such handsome fellows,"

she said. "Around here, they're rare as fish feathers."

They ate fast, and when Lillian brought the check, Jason saw she had written on it for Roy. "Bye, sweetheart!"

"Check the check," Jason warned. "Remember what Oscar told us."

"Looks right to me," Roy said. He left a good tip, then they slid out of the booth and walked out into the parking lot.

Just as Jason opened the passenger side door, he saw Lillian rushing toward them.

"Did we forget something?" Roy asked her.

"Me," she answered, a little out of breath.

Roy and Jason looked at her in confusion.

She put her head down as if needing to compose herself, and when she looked up again, her eyes were wet. "It's my mother," she said. "My poor old mom is dying—she's got the cancer bad. Real bad. My precious mother, she called me just now. Said she's feeling so awful-bad, she asked me to come be with her right now. I told my boss I've got to go now but, Roy, sweetheart, I don't have a car!" Lillian took a deep breath and continued, "I'd be thankful as a pilgrim if you'd drop me off at the Davenport Greyhound Station." Lillian opened her large black vinyl purse and pulled out a crumpled Kleenex to wipe her eyes.

"Lillian, ma'am, that's what we'll do. I believe it's on our way, so don't you worry. We'll get you there in no time."

Lillian patted Roy's wrinkled cheek. "You're a doll," she sniffled.

It was only twenty minutes to the bus station, yet Jason couldn't wait for her to get out of the car. He sat in the back seat while she sat up front talking and then giggling with Roy, amazing Jason by the speed with which she had perked up.

When they reached the bus station, Roy came around the side of the car and opened the door for her.

"Aren't you the gentleman!" she cooed. "Sweetheart, let me thank you proper-like."

While Jason got out to get in the front seat, she hugged Roy for what seemed to Jason a wrong amount of time. He turned away from them because he didn't even want to see it. When she finally let go of Roy, she walked toward Jason and ruffled his hair.

"Take care, cutie!" she sang. Then she turned and hurried toward the bus station entrance.

CHAPTER 21

"LILLIAN JUST WANTED A RIDE," JASON SAID QUIETLY. "She's full of shit."

Roy sighed. "Well, you're probably right but . . . I hope you're not."

"She flirted with you and you lapped it up."

"I did not!"

"You did. Like a cat laps up milk."

"Well, maybe I did . . . so what?"

"So, nothing," Jason said wearily. "But Roy, you're naïve! You need to be able to spot bad people right away!"

"I guess you're better at it than I am. Had more experience, huh?"

Jason didn't answer. He hated that Roy knew that he had a lot of experience with bad people and he could spot a phony a mile away. But he also knew that, for once in his life, he'd let it go.

"All I'm saying," Jason replied, "is that you can't let your guard down with people. Anyway, I'm glad she's gone. I didn't like her calling us those names and mussing my hair."

They got back in the car, and as Roy drove, they talked of other things and thought no more about Lillian.

On their way to Cleveland, a new idea uncurled in Jason's mind. They'd been racing across the country, seeing pretty much nothing. But what if, one day, he traveled the country slowly and saw things? He would travel this way one day, he thought. It was one thing to zoom through states seeing only rest stops and diners, and another thing to experience things. To *feel* things. To swim in rivers, walk the streets of New Orleans, Chicago, New York! To stand where history was made. But he'd never even seen a river or an ocean or any big city at all. So this was his new idea: one day, he would see the country for real . . . and maybe one day he'd see the country for real . . . *with Melanie.*

"You ever travel much?" he asked Roy.

Roy smoothed his hand over his head and said, "I was in Vietnam as a Marine and I traveled in Mexico and Europe with my wife."

Jason sat silent. Roy had been in Vietnam, and as a Marine! And Roy had once had *a wife*. Jason had forgotten that but now he remembered. "*Two years after my wife died . . .*" Jason was struck by the realization that he knew almost nothing about Roy's life because he had never cared to know.

Now he cared.

"I didn't know you were in Vietnam."

"'69 through '70."

"You must have seen a lot."

"A lot I'd rather not have seen . . . and rather not talk about."

"Sure," Jason said, and after thinking for a while, asked, "What was your wife like?"

"Pretty—light brown hair, dark brown eyes. She was quiet, certainly quieter than I am, yet she knew how to laugh, Nancy did. She laughed at my jokes, no matter how many times she heard them, and no matter how corny."

"Did she like science too?"

"Are you kidding? Nancy *was* a scientist. An anthropologist, and even wrote books on anthropology. She was a smart woman and as kind as can be. We couldn't have kids of our own, but Nancy loved every child in the neighborhood and they loved her." Roy paused, then chuckled. "Every Halloween, my Nancy would dress up as a Fairy Godmother and hand out a dollar bill and a candy bar to each trick-or-treater. Oh, she had fun doing that! She loved life, Nancy did." Roy stopped as if he was thinking of something else to say about her, but after some moments he just said, "I miss her."

"I can see," Jason said.

"After she passed away, I felt so lonely. It was like the loneliness I felt growing up those years with the Calverts. I always sensed something was missing, and what was missing was family. Real family—the kind that *feels* like family: heart-hurting and messy. Real family that misses you when you're not there and can make you cry simply because you love them and know you're so loved by them. Then, that day I got those documents in the mail and I learned that I had a brother! Well, that lifted me out of my loneliness. It was what I always wanted, yet learning of a brother who was nearly sixty years younger than me felt unholy."

"Creepy," Jason added.

"Yes, it is creepy, yet I wanted to find you. I knew I didn't want to die before I found you. I admit it was crazy the way I went about it, after you wouldn't answer my letters. I'm sorry about that now. I'm sorry I scared you that time. I didn't mean to scare you."

They were both silent for several moments, then Jason asked, "You said you wanted to help me piece together the fragments. What did you mean?"

"You remember that? Didn't think you were listening. Well, I meant that you were a fragment, like I was. A broken-off part. A part that didn't belong anywhere, didn't fit into a family. I didn't want you to feel like a fragment. It's a lonely feeling that I know too well. I didn't want you to be without real family even one more day than you had to. I wanted you to feel whole. Know where you came from and with whom you are blood-bonded. And that's what I want now for our brother . . . if he exists. I want him to know he has family. He has us. We'll piece together the fragments for him because he *belongs*."

While Roy was talking, Jason had that feeling again that Roy *knew* him. It was weird how the things Roy had felt growing up, *he* had felt. What Roy had longed for, *he* too had longed for. What's more, he saw that what Roy wanted, *he* wanted now as well.

"Then that's what we'll do," Jason said, his face feeling hot, his stomach tight with urgency. "If there's a kid out there, or soon will be, a kid who's our blood, then he belongs to us, and we belong to him. We won't let him be hurt or destroyed." He wanted to do for this kid, this . . . brother, what Roy had done for him. He suddenly knew he wanted to do that more than anything else in the world. "We'll save him, Roy. You and me. Together, we'll save him."

Roy glanced at Jason, surprised by his sudden fervor. "We'll do all we can," he replied, then looking back at the road ahead, said quietly, "No one can save him now but us, and if it happens, it was written in the stars."

CHAPTER 22

BY EARLY AFTERNOON, THEY REACHED CLEVELAND, where they stopped for gas and to change drivers. While Roy pumped the gas, Jason went into the fast food place next door to buy their lunch: a carton of milk for himself, coffee for Roy, and two hamburgers, then he stopped by the gas station's convenience store and bought a couple of oranges, and as a splurge: two chocolate bars. When Jason walked back to the car, he saw Roy peering under the driver's seat.

"What are you doing?"

"My wallet. Can't find it. I thought maybe it dropped under one of the seats."

Jason opened the passenger door, scooted the seat back, and searched the floor underneath.

Nothing.

Roy was still hunched over the driver's seat, staring downward, feeling around the tight spaces with his fingers. "Sometimes stuff slips between the seats," he said.

Jason heard the tension in Roy's voice. He removed the mats on the driver and passenger side, then examined the floor again.

Nothing.

Jason came around the side of the car to stand next to Roy.

"Where is it?" Roy asked the air.

"When did you last have it?"

"Well," Roy answered, nervously stroking his head. "I guess I had it last at the diner."

Then they knew.

"That waitress took my wallet!"

"She's a con artist," Jason spat. He'd had it right the first time. Roy was too trusting, and being too trusting was dangerous. "She was mugging you while hugging you!"

"Shit!" Roy snapped. "Shit!"

Jason never had heard Roy use that word, and dread rose within him. "What can we do?" he asked. "I've only got thirty-seven dollars left on my debit card and it'll be three days before more money comes in from Social Services."

"Nothing. There's *nothing* we can do. We're almost out of gas, and with gas prices as they are, your thirty-seven bucks won't get us to Ithaca, let alone buy us food."

Then, in a low, grief-stricken voice, he said, "I'm sorry, so sorry!"

"We've got to do *something*," Jason said. "We can't give up now! Maybe you can call someone—have them wire you money."

"Wouldn't help. My ID's gone too. To receive wired money, you need some ID, and besides, it could take twenty-four hours *at least* for the money to be wired."

"Call the police then. Tell them you got your wallet stolen."

"How's that going to help? They're not going to give us money."

"Then call the bank or let's get to a bank! Tell them you need money but don't have ID. Maybe they can do *something.*"

"Jason," Roy said, trying to keep his voice calm but

failing, "I will do that but it takes *at least twenty-four hours* to get another card, and again, *I have no identification*!"

Jason saw Roy's eyes wet with tears and said, "I'm not giving up. We're in this together, remember? I'm not giving up! Not yet. Not after we've come this far. We're *on a mission*, you and me. And this mission is a promise to our mother. It's like a *vow*."

A car honked behind them, so Roy went around and sat in the passenger seat and Jason drove the car away from the pump to the side of the gas station. When he turned the engine off, Roy leaned forward, rested his forehead on the dashboard, and wept. Jason gently put his hand on Roy's shoulder. He could feel the bony shoulder heaving as Roy sobbed, and he was reminded again of Roy's age and frailty and he felt a sharp stab of sadness.

"Maybe we could hitchhike," Jason gently suggested.

"No," Roy moaned between sobs. "Ithaca is more than three hundred miles away and most folks heading east aren't going *there*; they're going to Philadelphia or New York City." Roy wiped his eyes with his hand, sat back, and said gloomily, "We could wait hours and hours, maybe days for each ride we need to get to Ithaca, and besides, what would we do with this car?"

"I'll beg for the money," Jason declared. "I'll make a cardboard sign. I don't need to eat. We'll use the money I get for gas."

"Don't talk crazy. How much do you think you would make tonight to get us to Ithaca by tomorrow? And to get *around* Ithaca? And yes, you *do* need to eat. Begging isn't going to give us the money we need and it sure isn't going to give us the time."

"Wait!" Jason said. "Maybe we've got enough to take a bus to Ithaca?"

"Don't think so," Roy said, "but go see."

On his phone, Jason looked up: "Bus from Cleveland to Ithaca."

"It takes eight hours and would cost thirty-five dollars."

"Maybe," Roy considered, "we'd just make it."

Jason looked back at his phone "Oh, *per person.*"

Roy slumped back over the steering wheel, this time pressing his head hard against it as if the very force of his mind could transport them to Ithaca.

They sat silent while Jason's disappointment joined with anger and he started choking on the mixture. His heart raced. He wanted to hit something or someone hard. Wanted to scream. *I'd lock that Lillian in a cell,* he thought. *Bye, Sweetheart, I'd coo at her. I'd make her pay for what she's done to our dream. To our family.*

Yet Jason wanted something else— the one thing he wanted now more than he had ever wanted anything: to get himself and Roy to Ithaca by tomorrow night to save a possible sibling. That he could have a brother who might still be an embryo—such a possibility didn't seem crazy to him anymore. It seemed plausible, though just a tiny possibility. And that's what he wanted—this tiny possibility that had now vanished.

He drove to a nearby rest stop where, at a concrete picnic table, he handed Roy one of the hamburgers.

Roy shook his head. "Not hungry."

"It's pretty greasy, but still you need to eat," Jason said. "Here, at least have your coffee before it gets cold and have an orange and look—chocolate."

He handed the still-warm coffee and chocolate bar to Roy. Roy robotically drank the coffee and ate some of the hamburger, then absently nibbled the chocolate.

Jason ate his hamburger and drank the milk without tasting anything.

They got back in the car. The next stop would be the Citibank down the road, where Roy would report his credit card stolen.

As Jason buckled his seatbelt, he said more to himself than to Roy, "I wish we knew someone in Cleveland who could help us."

When Roy didn't respond, Jason looked over at him and saw something very wrong. Roy was slumped in the passenger seat with his head down almost to his groin.

"What are you doing?" Jason asked.

"Feeling weird," Roy said in a voice faint as smoke.

"What do you mean 'weird'?"

"Weak."

"You didn't get enough sleep."

"There's a pain too."

"A bad pain?"

"A bad pain."

"Where?"

Roy pointed to his chest.

"We've got to get you to the hospital."

"No," Roy said in a strained whisper. "We don't have time."

"What are you saying? We can't get to Ithaca by the deadline anyway. We don't have money, remember? And you yourself said it could be at least twenty-four hours before we could get some."

"Don't tell me what *I* said," Roy croaked. "Didn't *you* say we can't give up? Maybe we should go to the police station to see whether—"

"No. This is more important. You could be having a heart attack—we're going to the hospital."

Roy slumped sideways, resting his body against the passenger door as if he needed propping up and let out a quick cry of pain.

Jason Googled and found a hospital three miles away, leapt out of the car, came around the passenger side, fastened Roy's seat belt, then jumped back in the driver's seat, and with their last bit of gas, raced to it.

The emergency room was crammed with too many people and the place smelled like it. Some must have been waiting a good while because they'd fallen asleep.

The little end tables were littered with half-filled coffee cups and worn magazines. Babies cried, kids whined or ran around, and hovering over it all beamed some television game show with the sound turned off and the captioning on.

Roy, bent over in pain, walked as slowly as a mourner. His button-down blue shirt pressed against him, damp with sweat, and his face was clenched tight as a fist with pain. Jason helped him walk slowly to a chair. Then he went to the reception desk, where he explained the situation.

"He's got a bad pain in his chest and I think it could be a heart attack," Jason told the young woman. "He needs to be seen by a doctor—*quick.*"

The woman looked across the room at Roy. Jason was relieved to see concern in her eyes.

"When did this happen?" she asked.

"In the last few minutes."

"OK. I'll need his ID and health insurance."

"He lost it. He lost his wallet. Doesn't have ID. His name is Roy Calvert and I've got his social security number too."

The woman wrote it down, then asked, "Are you

related to Mr. Calvert?"

"I'm his grandson."

Within a minute, two men came out in scrubs and put Roy in a wheelchair. Jason followed as the big glass doors automatically swung open and they wheeled Roy deep into the emergency room.

A nurse took Roy's temperature and blood pressure, just before Dr. James Swedlow, tall, young, and sober-faced, checked Roy's heart. The nurse started an IV drip and Dr. Swedlow told Jason they'd need to run tests now on Roy.

"His blood pressure is elevated, 186 over 110. We're giving him nitroglycerin now to relax his blood vessels. This can restore blood flow to the heart in heart attack patients. And we'll need to run several tests to see what's going on."

"Don't need tests," Roy groaned but Jason and the doctor ignored him.

"How long will the tests take?" Jason asked.

"A few hours, but you don't need to wait here. You can take a walk, get something to eat. We have your cell phone number you gave the reception, so we'll text you when you can come back and see your grandfather."

"Can't I go with him to the tests?"

"Sorry, no. That's not allowed, but he should be finished in a few hours."

Jason turned back to Roy, who had been put on a gurney and was lying with his eyes closed, still as death, his arm attached to an IV.

"I'm OK," Roy said faintly as an orderly began to wheel him away toward the next set of double doors.

Jason watched in a kind of daze as the orderly pushed a wall button and the doors opened. Then he wheeled Roy's gurney through and the doors slowly wheezed shut behind them. And that's when Jason realized he hadn't said good-bye.

Jason stood in the emergency room for a moment as if in a stupor, until one of the nurses said, "Let me show you out."

Jason followed her, walked back into the waiting room and out the door of the hospital. He moved the car from the emergency parking space to the hospital parking lot, then got out and began walking aimlessly. The hospital complex was vast with several buildings separated by landscaping, small benches, and sculptures. The sky drooped over him, dark with rain clouds. The muggy air lay thick. Jason felt heavy and damp as well. He felt a weight in his chest and his legs felt sluggish too, as if he were walking through water. It seemed an effort to move but he wanted to keep moving, his body sluggish and his mind too—vague as water. Then he realized that tears were streaming down his face. Today, he'd lost the possibility of one sibling, and now he might lose Roy. *Roy!* The only family member he had and would ever have. Roy's life was in grave danger and there was nothing at all he could do about it.

"God," he prayed, "please don't let Roy die. He's all I've got. Please keep him for me. *Please.*"

With no direction, Jason just kept walking, but felt no longer part of the world around him. For the first time in his life, he knew he needed to talk to someone, to tell someone that he was hurting and that he was afraid. He needed to talk to someone who would not only understand, but would care.

He took out his phone, and through his tears, dialed her number.

CHAPTER 23

Pick up. Please, please pick up. Please, he silently begged.

"Hello?"

"Hi, Melanie," Jason said quietly.

"Jason? Is that you?"

"Yes."

There was silence on the other end and Jason could tell it wasn't a shy silence or a thinking silence. It was an angry silence.

"Melanie," Jason started. "Melanie, I. . . well . . . I want to talk with you."

The silence continued for another few moments, then she said, "You never answered my last texts. And you never called to tell me why . . . to tell me what's going on with you. I was worried about you."

Jason heard the hurt in her voice.

"But I did answer your texts. I swear I did. I *know* I did! And Melanie, I've been kind of busy. You see, I—"

"If you had replied to my texts, I would've gotten them," she countered. "And busy? What do you mean, busy?" she demanded. "And where've you been these past weeks? You left school so suddenly. Why? And why didn't you tell me?"

"Melanie, I wanted to but there was so much going on, and as I said, I know did answer your texts. Honestly, I did. And I thought about you all the time."

"Hah! Thanks for *thinking*."

"Look," Jason said, then stopped to stifle a cry. "I can explain everything. I mean, I will explain everything."

"When? Next year?"

"Now," Jason said.

"Well, if you want to explain things to me, you can meet me at Dougie's at six tonight and your explanation better be good."

"I can't meet you at Dougie's. I'm in Ohio. I'm at the Cleveland Midwest Hospital and things aren't going well . . . I'll probably be here for a few days, at least."

"You're in Cleveland and you're in the hospital?"

"Yeah, I'm in Cleveland, but no, *I'm* not in the hospital . . . a family member is."

"Family member? You told me you had no family! In fact, you told me that—"

"Melanie, please, I can explain. I promise you I will. But please try to understand,

I need you. I need to talk with someone. I mean I need to talk with *you.*"

"Great," Melanie said. "You lied to me about not having any family, you say you answered my texts, but you didn't. You completely ignored me until you need me now and you have the gall to expect me to be immediately available for a telephone chat with you. No thanks!"

Melanie hung up.

Jason felt hit in the chest by a hardball. He collapsed on the curb, cupping his head in his hands as his sobs sailed through the damp air. He couldn't stop crying and he didn't try, for he wanted to cry until his heart gave out. He was losing everything he ever cared about, and now loneliness wrapped around him like a shroud.

He took out his phone again and stared at the screen through his tears. His text messages from the last few days to Melanie had only been sent a few minutes ago. He remembered having to put the phone in airplane mode in the emergency room, yet still something had stopped the texts *before* that. Then he realized there may not have been cellular data at all in those rural parts of Illinois and Ohio they had driven through. He should have checked that!

Jason knew what he wanted to do, and for the first time in his life, he knew he could do it. He wiped his eyes and re-dialed her number but only got her voicemail, so he left a message, saying the words that so many times he had wished he could say.

"Melanie," he began, but then stopped, for he had let out a sob he hadn't wanted her to hear. Jason breathed slowly, and when he felt calmer, he continued in a voice raspy but steady. "Yes, you're right. I do need you now because I . . . I'm hurting so bad. I want to talk with you. Please, Melanie. Please believe me, because what I want to tell you is this: I need you, not just for now. What I'm saying is my heart's truth—I need you *in my life.* I love you, Melanie. I've always loved you, and I always will. Yes, you are the girl I love, Melanie, and *that's why* I need you. That's *how* I need you. I need you *always.*"

On his return to the hospital, Jason was told Roy had been moved to a room. When he entered the room, he saw Roy lying on his back asleep, hooked up to the electrocardiogram machine that monitored his heart and with a plastic oxygen tube in his nose. *He doesn't look good,* Jason thought, looking down at his brother, so frail and pale in his thin hospital gown. Jason sat in the big olive green vinyl chair next to the bed and for a long time just looked at Roy. It was five PM now, so why was Roy sleeping? And just when this question crossed his mind, Dr. Swedlow walked in.

"What's going on with him, Dr. Swedlow? Did he have a heart attack?"

"Well, we ran some tests on him—he did have elevated blood pressure and heart rate, but so far, we've found no evidence of a heart attack. But we need to run more tests. I'd rather he got some rest tonight and we'll get him tested in the morning." Dr. Swedlow glanced at Roy, then back at Jason. "Your grandfather looked pretty exhausted when we saw him in Emergency. He presented as depleted of energy. I'm sure you saw that."

"Yeah, but what about that bad pain in his chest?"

"Could be a number of things. A lot of things can mimic a heart attack—indigestion and some gastro-intestinal problems, such as ulcers and particularly heartburn—can all cause chest pain."

"I don't know what heartburn is," Jason admitted.

"It's a kind of indigestion caused when acid backs up. Certain foods cause it, like citrus fruits, chocolate, coffee, anything greasy. Do you know if your grandfather had anything like that before he came in?"

"Well, yeah, but would that be enough to cause such a bad pain?"

"Sure. The brain mixes up pain signals from the chest and the stomach. Sometimes," Dr. Swedlow added with a smile, "the brain's not as smart as we'd like. Besides, plain old stress can also give heart-attack-like symptoms. Your grandfather seemed to be under stress when you brought him in. Maybe something's been bothering him lately? Do you know of anything that might have caused him unusual stress?"

"I don't know," Jason said vaguely. "Does that mean he didn't have a heart attack?"

Dr. Swedlow focused his blue eyes on Jason, and

now Jason saw the concern that had always been there. "No, I'm not saying that. As I mentioned, we still have more tests to run and there are lab results we need back, so we won't know for certain what happened until later today or, most likely, tomorrow. In the meantime, we're monitoring him and giving him blood thinners, but just as important now, he needs to rest. He was somewhat agitated when you brought him in, so we gave him a mild sedative and that will help him get the rest he needs."

A male nurse came In to monitor Roy's vital signs as Dr. Swedlow continued.

"Jason, your grandfather may sleep right through suppertime, so I suggest you go home for now and come back tomorrow. You look like you could use some rest yourself. After all, the night nurse will be checking on him regularly and I'll be back tomorrow in the early afternoon, following his tests."

"We're not from Cleveland; we've been traveling. I don't want to leave him alone, so I'll just sleep here, if that's all right."

"You can do what you want, but you'll have a challenge trying to sleep in that chair."

"I'll be OK."

"Suit yourself. I'll ask the nurse to bring you some dinner."

The hours dragged on. Roy did not wake and Jason did not sleep. He just watched Roy sleep. Jason felt Roy was distant from him now—in another world, which he could not enter. Watching Roy lie still as stone and hearing the intermittent beeping of the heart monitor just enlarged his fear that Roy could die, so he kept his eyes on Roy, as if his very gaze could pin Roy to life.

Around midnight, Jason at last fell asleep, dozing fitfully until just before dawn, when he was wakened by Roy's voice.

"What the hell . . . ?"

"Roy!" Jason stood up at the side of the bed and looked down at him.

"Who put me in this darn nightgown!"

"You're in the hospital. You had a bad chest pain yesterday and they're running tests on you."

"Well, I don't have pain now. I'm fine."

"Good. Dr. Swedlow says they need to do more tests on you later today. And he said you need your rest, so you should go back to sleep."

"Sleep? I already slept. I need to get out of here. Hospitals are dangerous—loaded with germs and mysterious smells and they serve you kindergarten food: milk in little cartons and Jell-O cubes. Let's go."

Roy pulled the oxygen cord from his nose, then started removing the electrocardiogram patches from his chest.

"Stop!" Jason cried, grabbing his arm, but it was too late.

Roy had already scooted over to the other side of the bed and was now standing on the linoleum floor, looking confused. "Where'd they put my clothes?"

"Roy, you're being unreasonable. Please get back in bed. You need to get tests done to see what's going on with your heart! Please, Roy," Jason pleaded. *Please.*"

"Sorry, Jason, but I don't like hospitals and, oh, there we are." Roy had opened the narrow closet and saw the white plastic bag with his clothes and shoes inside. He pulled it out and headed for the bathroom, but Jason blocked him and grabbed the bag. They tussled over it for some moments but Roy, realizing he didn't have the strength to take it from Jason, exclaimed in exasperation, "Give it back! I want to put my clothes on and feel human again. And besides," Roy said, pointing to the young woman who had appeared in the doorway, "this arguing is no doubt frightening the nice nurse over there."

Jason turned to where Roy was pointing.

"I'm not a nurse," Melanie said.

CHAPTER 24

In that dreamlike moment in which Jason, speechless, stared at Melanie in her red parka as if she were an apparition, Roy grabbed the plastic bag and ducked into the bathroom.

"I don't understand," Jason stammered. "I thought you were angry."

"I was," Melanie said as she walked toward him, "but then I realized you must be in some kind of trouble . . . some kind of pain and," she said with a smile, standing beside him, "I liked your voice message."

Jason gently pulled her toward him and kissed her. Her mouth was so warm, the caress of her lips softer than he could have even imagined. Their kisses, at first delicate and delicious, turned heated and hungry. They held each other tightly, kissing again and again. Jason smelled that good flower smell of her.

"I love you," he whispered, nestling the words into her neck.

He had said the word, and in the saying of it, the fear and anger he had felt all his life at the word fell away, like clothes that no longer fit. Love now was like a beginning thing—like learning to walk—and he knew he could do it, and he knew too that the hurt so deep within him was gone, maybe forever.

Finally, reluctantly, Jason released Melanie, but not before she embraced him one more time as she murmured, "I love you, Jason. I think I always have and I know I always will."

Jason cupped Melanie's face in his hands and peered into her blue eyes.

They smiled happily at each other then, kissed yet again, both not wanting to stop.

"Pardon me," Roy whispered as if not wanting to wake someone.

"Oh," Jason said, stepping back. "Melanie, this is Roy. Roy Calvert. Roy, this is Melanie Sandersborn."

"Nice to meet you, Mr. Calvert," Melanie said, extending her hand.

"Nice to meet *you*, young lady," Roy said. "Jason's told me about you."

"He has?"

"Sure, He told me about your report on ignition systems . . . and I suspect," Roy added with a grin, "you sure seem able to ignite *him*."

"Look, Roy," Jason said after this embarrassing comment. "A nurse could come in any minute, so please get back in the bed."

"No, I won't. I want to leave now while troops are thin on the ground. Besides, I need a decent breakfast, and perhaps with our last reserves of cash, we could even treat this young lady."

Jason, finally understanding Roy's determination to leave, knew further argument would be useless.

"Mr. Calvert," said Melanie, "If you leave a hospital without the hospital's permission, you need to sign a form saying you don't hold them responsible for what happens to you."

"Melanie, you can call me Roy, and you've got a good point." Roy reached inside the plastic bag, grabbed the paper on which the nurse had listed his clothes and turned it over. With a pen Melanie handed him, he wrote:

I'm leaving. I feel good. The Cleveland Hospital is not liable for anything that should befall me.

—Roy Calvert

Roy grinned as he lay the note on the pillow. "I like that word, 'befall.'"

They stuck their heads outside the room. Only two nurses were at the nurses' station and they were chatting with each other, their backs turned. Roy, Jason, and Melanie carefully walked to the door that led down the stairs, went down one flight, then took the elevator to the lobby. Roy waited with Melanie in front of the hospital until Jason brought the car around. Then they were gone.

CHAPTER 25

AT 3:30 IN THE MORNING, THE CHICKEN AND EGG Diner off Interstate 90 outside Cleveland was pretty empty, just three truck drivers hunched at the counter. Jason slid into a booth. Roy sat beside him and Melanie opposite.

"OK," Melanie said, after they'd ordered. "What's going on?"

"You see," Jason started, "it's kind of a long story."

"I'm listening."

Jason glanced at Roy, then back at Melanie. "I found my family."

"Wonderful! You mean you found your birth mother?"

"Yeah."

"Have you met her yet?"

"I can't."

"Why not?"

"She's dead."

"Jason, I'm so sorry. I'm sorry you didn't get a chance to meet her."

"I couldn't have met her," Jason said, "because . . . because . . .she died before I was born."

Melanie's face went pale as she murmured, "Oh, in childbirth."

"No. She died seventy-five years ago." There, he'd said it. He'd told her this crazy-ass thing.

"I don't understand," Melanie said. "What you just said isn't possible."

Jason sighed. "It's possible."

As Roy quietly picked at his waffle, Jason explained it to her and more—about his mother being a concert cellist, the frozen embryos, Dr. Ernst Fritzhauer, the plane crash, but he hadn't yet explained who Roy was, nor mentioned a triplet. Could he tell her these wild things? Or would they sound more than impossible to her? Sound abnormal? Unnatural? Repulsive? Jason felt, yet again, how different he was without a mom and a dad. Ironically, now he had found his family, the circumstances of his family marked him as even *more* different. Downright weird. He wouldn't blame Melanie if she didn't believe him. He wouldn't blame her if she thought she was being kidded. He wouldn't blame her if she laughed at his story, was repelled by it, or even if she got up and left.

"There's more to tell, isn't there?" Melanie asked, "That's not all, is it?"

Jason stared into his glass of orange juice, while he heard Roy say under his breath, "No, not all."

"Roy's my brother," Jason said in a rush. "My identical twin."

He took a long gulp of the orange juice. Melanie looked at Roy in surprise as silence fell over the table like a sound.

After several moments, Melanie said, "I thought perhaps Roy was your uncle." She looked back at Jason and smiled. "I understand now."

"You're a perceptive person," Roy told her.

Jason looked back at Melanie and saw in her face no shock, no repugnance, no disbelief. Melanie believed him and she understood. Jason wanted to lean across the table and kiss her. He wanted to thank her for being all he had yearned for.

"But," Melanie, said slowly, looking first at Jason, then at Roy. "There's something else, isn't there? I think there's something sad between you two and you still haven't told me why you're here. What are you doing in Cleveland? Do you live here, Roy?"

So, Roy and Jason, sometimes talking over one another, explained about the third embryo and the documents sent to Roy and their mother's secret letter, which Jason had decoded, and the frozen embryo clinic in Ithaca. They told her they thought the third embryo might still exist at this clinic, so they had wanted to find their brother before the deadline or he would be destroyed.

Though the information was as wild as science-fiction, Melanie calmly ate the last bite of her omelet and said, "I'm tired, and I see you both are too, but forgive me, I have to know more."

"Ms. Melanie," Roy said. "You've come all this way on a red-eye for us; you have a right to know anything you want."

"Go ahead," Jason said to Melanie. "What more would you like to know?"

Melanie pushed her plate to the side and leaned over the table toward them.

"I want to know why you couldn't have just called this clinic from Clearview to get the information?"

"We didn't have a number for it. There'd once been a number but we called it and it wasn't a working number. We couldn't find a working phone number now," Jason answered. "No website either."

"Don't you think then," Melanie asked in a tone both patient and skeptical, "that it's probably because the clinic no longer exists?"

"Could very well be," Roy said, "but we felt we owed it to our sibling to come here in person and find out whatever we could. Even if the clinic doesn't exist, maybe if we ask around we'll find someone who worked there and might know something—any little bit of information that could be helpful."

"I see," Melanie said, slowly twisting a strand of her long hair. "But even if the place still exists, aren't the odds pretty slim that this clinic would have kept an embryo for this long? I mean, what if this embryo, your brother, was already born years ago? Maybe he's now forty, or sixty?"

"We thought of that," Jason said. "If that happened, then the clinic might have the information where we could find him."

Melanie pressed on. "And what if your triplet isn't identical? What if it's a girl? I mean, triplets are so rare, and I would think identical triplets even more rare."

Roy and Jason looked at each other. A girl? They hadn't thought of that.

"That would be OK," Roy said. "Wouldn't change a thing."

"We would still want to find her," Jason said sadly, as much to himself as to Melanie. "To know whether our sister is alive."

"OK, now here's my last question—who were you planning to carry the embryo if the embryo existed? Someone would have to carry it to term."

"The Kramers," Jason said.

"The Kramers? You mean—your foster family?"

"Yeah. I mean, I feel bad how I ignored them. I was messed up and couldn't see their goodness, but I can now. They're kind and they wanted a baby but thought they were too old to adopt one. They aren't too old at all! They could take our brother or sister and would love the baby. I'm sure of it."

"Did you ask them?"

"I sent them an email explaining everything, but I haven't talked to them yet. I already researched it. We could ship the embryo in liquid nitrogen with FedEx by what they call a dry shipment to a clinic that reports to the Society of Reproductive Medicine, and I found one in Reno. It's where they do the implantation, called an FET, a frozen embryo transfer."

"Did they reply?"

"Well . . . not yet . . ."

"Were you OK with this, Mr. Calvert?"

"Melanie, you can call me Roy, and you bet I'm OK with it. If our sibling has a loving mother and father from the get-go, it's more than Jason and I had, and it's what we want for the child. We talked it over, and if the clinic could release the embryo to the Kramers, and if Mrs. Kramer could bring it to term, our prayers would be answered."

"But," Melanie asked, "what if they don't want to? And if Mrs. Kramer's too old to bear a child, you'll need a surrogate."

Jason and Roy looked at each other. Melanie was posing questions they should have answered days ago.

They'd never thought of what would happen if the Kramers didn't or couldn't take the embryo. Fear filled Jason's heart. The deadline for destruction was today. What would they do? A frozen embryo would die within hours if not implanted into a woman of child-bearing age.

"If they can't or won't," Roy said softly, his lower lip trembling just a bit, "our quest to save our triplet will end. It will end in our failure . . . and our triplet's death, and we'd have to live with our failure for the rest of our lives."

"You see," Jason explained as Roy took out his handkerchief and wiped his eyes, "this has been a long way of telling you why we're here and where we were heading. But it's all a bust. It's all a bust and now we have to live with this failure for the rest of our lives."

Melanie's face became pale as paper. "There's something else," she said firmly. "There's something bad and sad. Something wrong . . . I feel it from both of you. There's something else you haven't told me." She kept her eyes on Jason as she spoke.

Jason glanced at Roy, who nodded wearily, drooped as a limp plant.

"Roy got his wallet stolen yesterday," Jason said. "And I can't get more money for another two days and we're almost out of gas and we haven't even gone to the bank yet and . . . well, anyway, we don't—"

"You don't have the money to get to Ithaca," Melanie confirmed matter-of-factly. "But when you get the money, you can go!"

"No," Roy said so quietly, he could barely be heard, "We can't."

"Melanie," Jason said, "the hospital delay and the money thing—there's no way we could make the deadline now."

"When's the deadline?"

"Today."

Melanie took in a little breath, then she took out her phone.

"What are you doing?" Jason asked.

"Seeing how long it would take to drive from here to Ithaca. Oh, here it is—five hours, a pretty straight shot on Highway 90, then 86. Let's go!"

"Our mother stipulated that the deadline is noon," Jason said. "We can't make it."

Melanie again glanced at her phone. "It's 6:30, so even stopping for gas, if there's no rush hour traffic, we might get there by noon . . . it's worth a try."

"But we don't have—"

"I have money. You can pay me back when you get some. Let's go!"

She took cash out of her wallet, and as she did, Jason thought how remarkable she was. How her words could be as strong as Oscar's punches and as soft as the notes from his harmonica.

"I'm with you," she announced to Roy and Jason, "all the way with you."

Roy, who had suddenly become energized, asked, "What do you mean?"

"I mean, I'm not just paying for you to get to Ithaca. I'm coming with you, and if there's some clinic, I'm going inside with you."

"You don't need to—" Jason started.

"Yes, I do. This is important, and I meant it that I'm there for you. And I don't know exactly how, but I feel I'm supposed to be here. Like I can help or something. I mean," she added with a sly smile, "I am the one with the dough."

Roy smiled back at her. "You're right, Melanie. You have the money and the moxie. We're grateful and in your hands."

CHAPTER 26

JASON DROVE THEM TO THE ADDRESS ON DR. ERNST Fritzhauer's old 1950 letterhead: 756 Keeler Street. When he turned off the engine, it was 11:27.

As they were parking, the storm broke. The sky became a black blanket. The streets gave off the smell of asphalt and damp dirt. Dogs howled as thunder cracked like a whip over the city and rain beat down in a sudden, fierce torrent.

The three hurried up the steps of an immense brick house that didn't look like a clinic but some old, neglected residence, huge in size and the color of dirt, with blinds drawn and with neither welcome mat nor doorbell. They knocked on the door but got no answer.

"This doesn't seem right," Jason said nervously, and Roy and Melanie's silence confirmed his impression.

"Maybe we should ask someone," Melanie suggested.

They looked up and down the water-filled streets to see only one pedestrian, a man rushing along, unhappily stepping into the swirling sidewalk water while struggling to keep his umbrella upright in the angry wind.

Jason ran down the steps and approached the man.

"Excuse me," he said, pointing to the house and shouting to be heard above the thunder, "do you know whether this is the Fritzhauer Clinic?"

"Don't involve yourself!" the man yelled.

"I just want to know if—"

"Go away!" the man yelled as he hurried down the flooding street.

Soaking wet, Jason ran back up the steps of the house, where Melanie and Roy stood dry under the eave.

"What did he say?" Melanie asked.

"I didn't understand him," Jason said.

Thunder exploded like a bomb over the streets, while for several seconds, the sky was lit bright by lightning, as if some celestial switch had been flicked.

"With this racket," Roy said, "whoever's inside isn't going to hear our knocking."

"I see a doorbell!" Melanie cried, pointing to a dark bumpy knob beside the mail slot.

Yes, there it was. A metal button set inside the mouth of a carved iron demon face. The face was no bigger than a quarter and so intricately molded that it appeared malevolent with its pointed ears, fangs, a grisly leer and sockets rather than eyes.

"Left over from Halloween," Roy muttered as he pushed the doorbell button inside the demon's gaping mouth. Then, in a tense pause between the thunder, they heard from inside the sound of unhurried footsteps approaching.

"May I help you?" a tall, thin man asked, holding the door open only a crack as he peered at them.

"If you're a doctor at the Fritzhauer clinic," Roy said, "we'd like to speak with you."

"Well, yes indeed, I am that doctor," the man replied, opening the door a few inches wider.

He was in his forties, with pale blue eyes, angular features as if chiseled in stone, and a full head of graying brown hair. He looked elegant in his black turtleneck sweater, pale gray sports jacket, and black slacks.

"My name is Dr. Andrew Fritzhauer. May I ask of what nature is your visit?"

"We're here on a mission," Roy explained. "We are family to one of the embryos that might be in your clinic."

The man gave an abrupt smile, like a knife flashing. "A mission! That sounds important. Please come in and let me know how I may help you."

They stepped into a long, dimly-lit hallway and were led into a living room, also dimly lit.

"Janet!" the man called into another room. "We have three guests, please bring coffee." Then, turning to his visitors, Dr. Fritzhauer said good-naturedly, "Please be seated so we can have a little talk."

After they sat down, Jason asked, "Are you related to Dr. Ernst Fritzhauer?"

"Ernst Fritzhauer was my grandfather. I revered him for his pioneering work which, after his death, my father carried on. Sadly, my father died six years ago, so now I have the honor of continuing the important work of the Fritzhauer Clinic, though with a quite different, as you would say, *mission*."

"Well, Dr. Fritzhauer," Roy began, "we're glad to have found you. We've come because we have a responsibility toward one of the embryos we believe was frozen—frozen in time—by your grandfather. We would like to know what ever happened to that embryo? Specifically, if, by chance, it might still exist?"

As Roy explained further, Jason looked around the room. At first, he thought the room was dark from the storm outside but now he noticed the heavy blue drapes drawn across the windows and the inadequate light from a table lamp in the corner. The room was orderly, yet there was nothing to suggest it was a clinic. It had nothing medical about it or even office-like. It was merely a living room, exuding a mingled smell of milk and must, and sparsely furnished with a bulky sofa on which he, Melanie, and Roy sat, a spindly chair holding Dr. Fritzhauer, and an overstuffed armchair that seemed to skulk in the shadows like an animal. Three small tables dotted the room with nothing placed atop them, except the one beside the sofa, which held a book. A single picture graced the walls: a large portrait of the same inhuman face as on the doorbell.

"Intriguing story!" the man enthused when Roy

paused. "Tell me more."

"Nothing more to tell, really," Roy said. "We have the documents to prove our relationship to the embryo that was kept here— letters from our mother, letters from your grandfather and from the doctors who arranged our births, one of whom was my father. We also have Jason's and my DNA reports."

"Excellent!" the man said cheerily.

As Roy opened the large leather envelope, he said, "We are most curious about why our mother believed there were three embryos but the documents my father bequeathed to me inform of only two. We want to know why and we want to know—"

Roy was interrupted by the banging open of the kitchen door and the entrance of a thin, young woman bearing a wooden tray with a green china coffee service. The woman walked stiffly, dressed in jeans and a soiled, barrel-shaped sweater. Her dull-brown hair was pulled severely back into a ponytail and tied with a worn athletic shoelace. The woman's pallid face was narrow as a rodent's and her eyes seemed to look at things without seeing them. The doctor made no attempt to introduce her. She set the tray down on the coffee table in front of the sofa, poured the coffee, then silently handed each person a cup and saucer. As she did this, they heard, from the kitchen, the mewling of a cat. Then she left the room and walked back toward the kitchen as robotically as she had entered.

Jason sipped the coffee, and as he did, his eye fell on the book on the table beside him: *World Progress through Leadership of the Determined*, by Dr. Andrew Fritzhauer. The cover image was of the universe superimposed over the demon face.

The cat yowled in the kitchen, the wind howled in the chimney, and hail pounded the roof, forcing Dr. Fritzhauer to speak loudly. In his measured voice, he explained to them the clinic's mission.

"The clinic my grandfather founded was built on helping families have children. Indeed, he called it his 'frozen orphanage.' However, when I took over the clinic, I developed what I believe to be a worthier goal—that of promoting human progress and purity. I confess my lack of modesty when I say, under my leadership, the clinic now has an exalted mission. We undertake not to help just families, but to help, I daresay, *save* humanity. And we are no longer accountable to any authority but the authority of what we deem to be the Determined."

"Pardon me for interrupting," Roy said, "but I don't understand what you mean."

Dr. Fritzhauer smiled indulgently at Roy as if Roy were an insistent child. "What I *mean*," Dr. Fritzhauer said, "is that those of us who labor for the clinic, are determined to advance humanity by selecting embryos from our remaining embryos, the frozen, the forgotten, the forsaken. We choose to raise these as leaders of the New World Order of the Determined."

"I still don't understand—" Roy started, but Melanie, who had been fidgeting edgily in her seat, now interrupted.

"What about the *parents* of these embryos?"

"Young lady, often the parents of the embryos have since passed away or simply are no longer interested in parenthood. Unfortunate for them, perhaps, but not for us. By rescuing these pre-formed humans, we will be empowered to form them. They will be raised to rescue the world. You see, we have rescued them and they will, in return, rescue us."

Jason looked hard into Dr. Fritzhauer's eyes. He felt

tense as a tiger when he heard Melanie ask another question.

"May I ask whose face is on the doorbell and in that picture on the wall?"

"Natas," the doctor answered. "More precisely, it is a depiction of my interpretation of the being we perceive as most liberated from dogma and human deficiency. I gave him this name myself, and I admit his image at first glance may appear as one of malevolence. In truth, though, he is a symbol of our misunderstood, yet righteous struggle for freedom and we—"

"You're an *author!*" Jason suddenly cried.

"And *you* are an observer!" Dr. Fritzhauer chuckled. "Yes, I've written one book, but I am far from famous."

"Even one book is quite an accomplishment," Melanie said.

"What do you write about?"

Jason took out his phone.

"I write," Dr. Fritzhauer explained, "about my philosophy of the Determined, a philosophy which is now integral to the clinic."

"Do you mind if I take your photo? Jason asked,

"We've traveled such a long way to get here and we want to create a photo book of our trip. I'd be grateful If I could take a photo of you, since you and the clinic are so important to our family. Besides, it would be nice to have a photo of a real author."

"I don't mind at all," Dr. Fritzhauer said as he stood up. "Indeed, I am happy to grant your small request as our families are unquestionably entwined. Shoot away, young man."

Jason swiped the phone's screen and pressed buttons while Dr. Fritzhauer posed. Jason walked around him to capture him from different angles.

"I'm sorry, but there's not much light here, yet it's a bit better from this side," Jason explained, and as the doctor good-naturedly pivoted around, he tapped the camera button repeatedly.

"I feel quite the celebrity!" crowed Dr. Fritzhauer.

"I don't think we should keep Dr. Fritzhauer from his important work," Roy protested. Jason ignored him.

"But Jason," Melanie said excitedly as she stood up, "Dr. Fritzhauer's best side is *this* one. Please, Dr. Fritzhauer, would you mind turning just a bit to the right. And again to the right?" Working like a team,

Jason and Melanie directed Dr. Fritzhauer's turns as Jason shot dozens of photos.

Growing yet more irritated, Roy said, "Jason! We're keeping the good doctor from his important work."

"YOU ARE NOT KEEPING ME FROM ANYTHING!" Dr. Fritzhauer cried loudly as if in a trance, "SHOOT ME! SHOOT AWAY!" The doctor's booming voice startled them.

It had so abruptly become disengaged and frenzied—as if he had, in an instant, borrowed a lunatic's voice and was now playing with it. "SHOOT ME! SHOOT AWAY!" he cried again.

When Jason had photographed Dr. Fritzhauer from every possible angle, he sat back down and the doctor, like a programmed thing, returned to his composed manner.

"I beg your forgiveness," he said. "I have been talking about myself and our work, when you have come a long way, and as you say, on *a mission*. I would be remiss if right this minute I did not check our registry to find the embryo to which you are referring and to answer the questions as why your father may never have referred to a third one. I need to identify its drawer—that is our clinic's term for an embryo's freezing compartment—and learn its history and current status. Would you kindly excuse me?"

"Of course," Roy replied eagerly, "by all means."

After Dr. Fritzhauer left the room, Roy turned angrily to Jason, "Stop engaging him in conversation. And enough with the pictures! Why on Earth do you want so many pictures of him anyway?"

Jason did not answer.

"Fine! Be rude all you want, but we came here to find out something important."

Roy stared hard at Jason and Melanie as he said, "Let's all *focus*."

The violence of the storm rattled the windows. As they waited, Melanie picked up the doctor's book, and after reading for a minute, whispered. "Listen!" She read to them aloud:

"The current vision of 'family life' has robbed humanity of its autonomy. Family life is nothing but a selfish sham. It has been disastrous for the evolution of the human race. I argue that there needs to be a self-direction of human evolution. The World Order of the Determined is founded on the principle that, by

procuring embryos, we can, without the detrimental effects of parenting, incubate a new and hardier human race, prepared to dominate and triumph over the fraudulent virtues of weakness, sentimentality and love."

"He's a whack-job," Jason said.

"He's an odd duck, that's for sure," Roy said. "But what he does with his clinic is his business. Our business is our triplet. We don't need to like or even understand this guy, we just need to just get information."

"But he could harm others," Melanie argued. "His ideas are sick. And don't you see what you get when you spell NATAS backwards?"

Roy stayed firm. "We need to focus on *why* we're here. Besides, we can't do anything about his nutty ideas."

"We can go to the police," Melanie said.

"No," Jason said. "Roy's right. We need to find out first if—"

Jason stopped as Dr. Fritzhauer re-entered the room, his face mournful. He sat down in one of the old green armchairs opposite them and spoke in a low voice. "Mr. Calvert, your father never mentioned the third embryo simply because he knew his wife would not want to bear, let alone raise, *three* children. Indeed, our records indicate she agreed to bear only one of the embryos. Your father retained the second one, in the hope of soon convincing her to bear another. However, the third embryo, my grandfather kept in the clinic, as no doubt he thought he might eventually offer it to a childless couple. The record also indicates that your father agreed to my grandfather keeping it, but only if this embryo transfer would remain confidential. I gather that your mother's long-ago letter now has broken this confidentiality."

Roy, Melanie and Jason sat quiet at this information, while the doctor continued in a somber voice. "Additionally, I regret to inform you, as you may have already known, that the freezing process is not foolproof. There are several inherent risks. And as such, it is painful for me to inform you that I checked our database and looked for the status of Drawer Number 12428, the one with your triplet. I learned that this embryo was unable to survive cryopreservation, which is what we call the long freezing state." The doctor swiveled his flat-as-glass eyes on Roy's grief-stricken face. "It was posthumously recorded as male, and sadly, it was destroyed twenty-three years ago. I am terribly sorry to disappoint you, especially because I understand the distance you have traveled, and more than that, the deep emotions involved."

Jason stood and walked to stand in front of the doctor. "You're lying," he said.

"Jason, please," Roy said, walking over to him and putting his hand on Jason's shoulder to calm him. "You don't know that."

Jason shrugged off Roy's hand as he continued to stare down at Dr. Fritzhauer.

"I'm used to people lying to me," he said quietly. "I can smell a lie like a dog smells shit. You're lying."

Dr. Fritzhauer stood up and looked back at Jason with eyes cold as death. "I am afraid you are wrong," he said, "and I think it best you all leave now."

Roy and Melanie turned to go, but Jason didn't move. He kept his eyes on Dr. Fritzhauer as he seemed to listen to something.

"Come, brother," Roy said, "we did all we could . . ."
Jason bolted toward the kitchen. Panicked, Melanie

and Roy ran after him.

"JANET! WATCH OUT!" Dr. Fritzhauer shouted as the three burst into the dank kitchen and immediately gagged from the combined stench of sour milk, coffee, and urine.

At the side of a dirty stove, the woman, Janet, cowered in the corner, rocking back and forth on her haunches and in a rasping voice like a buzzer, sang, *"Don't want it. Don't hurt me. Don't want it, Don't hurt me, Don't want it, Don't hurt me . . ."*

Then, there, atop a pile of foul-smelling laundry on the kitchen counter, they saw it—the newborn baby boy, wrinkled as a raisin, making pathetic kitten-like cries from hunger. The exhausted infant futilely jerked its arms about.

That's how they spotted on its right forearm the tiny hammer-shaped birthmark.

CHAPTER 27

"OUR BROTHER," CRIED ROY, "THAT'S *HIM!*"

"You're mistaken," Dr. Fritzhauer barked. "He is ours, and he has a role in life that we have assigned him." He picked up the infant roughly, but it was too weak to cry now. Around the child's foot was a band with writing, which Dr. Fritzhauer read:

"Born <August 28, 2026> Drawer # 12428

Female Carrier: Janet

Lifetime Rescue Responsibility: General Laborer for the Determined.

"You see," he said, his eyes wild with triumph, "whoever he may have once belonged to, he has been with us seventy-five years, so obviously he is *ours.* May I remind you: Possession is nine-tenths of the law."

"GIVE US OUR BROTHER!" Roy shouted. "OR

I'LL SEND YOU TO HELL!"

The doctor glared like a wolf at Roy as he held fast to the baby.

"I was too nice to you," Dr. Fritzhauer said, shooting his words like bullets. "I gave you shelter and coffee on this wretched day, yet when I asked you to leave, you disobeyed. You had all better go. Right *now*."

"We're not leaving," Jason stated. "We're not going without our brother. Your ways are evil and we won't leave him with you!"

"I rather think you *are* leaving," Dr. Fritzhauer replied in an ice-hard voice. With one hand he tossed the baby back onto the pile of laundry and with the other withdrew a handgun from his inner jacket pocket and pointed it at the child.

"*Don't want it. Don't hurt me. Don't want it. Don't hurt me. Don't want it. Don't hurt me . . .*" Janet chanted louder.

"SHUT UP!" With the gun still aimed at the baby's head, Dr. Fritzhauer walked over to the crouching woman in the corner and kicked her hip. She did not cry out but simply continued to sing her pathetic lament.

"We have many more embryos, and Janet here could bear a dozen for us with no birth records at all," Dr. Fritzhauer said. "If you get the police or cross me in any way, I will destroy this runt. I have no qualms about doing it. He is a nobody without a birth certificate, who will never be known or remembered. And in this weakling's place, I will order another forgotten embryo to be born. And this new youth will grow up and the world will tremble before him. A youth that must and will fearlessly bear pain. Yes, our youth will be all that—nothing weak and gentle. A free, splendid beast of prey must flash from its eyes. *That* is how I will promote the eradication of thousands of years of human domestication. *That* is how I will create the New Order of the Determined."

"FAKER! MADMAN! CRIMINAL!" Roy yelled as he rushed at Dr. Fritzhauer.

"NO!" screamed Melanie as Dr. Fritzhauer, with one hand, shoved Roy so hard, Roy fell backwards to the floor.

Melanie leapt forward to help Roy stagger to his feet.

"ENOUGH!" roared Dr. Fritzhauer, his face red

with rage. "ENOUGH! I WARNED YOU NOT TO CROSS ME. TRAITORS! I NOW SEE THAT ALL OF YOU, INCLUDING THIS BASTARD BABY, ARE UNFIT FOR MANKIND. I NEED TO REMEDY THIS." He held the newborn at arm's length as if it were a repulsive thing and pointed the gun at the baby's head.

But an instant before that, Jason pressed a button on his phone.

CHAPTER 28

"SHOOT ME! SHOOT AWAY! SHOOT ME! SHOOT AWAY! SHOOT ME! SHOOT AWAY! SHOOT ME! SHOOT AWAY! SHOOT ME! SHOOT AWAY! SHOOT ME! SHOOT AWAY!" cried the twelve Dr. Fritzhauers in unison.

"SHOOT ME! SHOOT AWAY! SHOOT ME! SHOOT AWAY! SHOOT ME! SHOOT AWAY! SHOOT ME! SHOOT AWAY! SHOOT ME! SHOOT AWAY! SHOOT ME! SHOOT AWAY! SHOOT ME! SHOOT AWAY!"

The human-sized images, real as life, smiled and pivoted, spinning around Dr. Fritzhauer like demon embodiments of himself. Their chorus of cries was earsplitting and the sight of them, so horribly lifelike with their gray jackets, perfectly creased black slacks, phony smiles, and flashing eyes, immobilized Dr.

Fritzhauer. He stood frozen, utterly terrorized by the screaming avatars of his evil self.

"SHOOT ME! SHOOT AWAY! SHOOT ME! SHOOT AWAY! SHOOT ME! SHOOT AWAY! "HOOT ME! SHOOT AWAY! SHOOT ME! SHOOT AWAY! SHOOT ME! SHOOT AWAY!"

As the dank kitchen boomed and echoed with this now insane request, Melanie leapt forward and grabbed the baby.

"RUN!" she screamed. "RUN!"

She grabbed Roy's hand. Roy, hobbling in pain, hurried with her as best he could. Melanie pulled him out of the kitchen, through the living room and down the dark hallway.

"HURRY!" she shouted back to Jason. "C'MON!"

"GET THE BABY TO THE HOSPITAL!" Jason cried after them. "HURRY!" But Jason did not follow, for Fritzhauer, his face disfigured with rage, was standing, aiming the gun at him.

It seemed that, in that millisecond, Jason was aware of a thousand sounds around him. The wind ripping through the trees outside the kitchen window. Janet's weeping. A loud car horn. The boom of thunder again.

Fritzhauer was not a man to point a gun and fail to shoot.

Fritzhauer did shoot, but not before Jason dove to the floor, then leapt forward, knocking Fritzhauer off balance so that he toppled to the floor like a bowling pin. Jason reached for the gun. Fritzhauer grabbed it first and raised it—but Jason punched him hard in the stomach. The crazed man rolled over and groaned, still holding fast to the gun. Jason's mind locked into sharp focus. With no time to unleash more terrifying holograms, he grabbed the metal coffee pot and hurled it at Fritzhauer, smashing it into his head just as the gun went off again, blasting into the wall, making the weeping woman howl like a witch.

In the seconds before Fritzhauer could stand again, Jason turned and ran from the house as the madman's screams rocketed through it.

Outside in the rain, Jason hoped he wouldn't see Roy or Melanie. That baby was near death and they couldn't have waited but a minute for Jason before needing to race to the hospital. No sign of them. Their car was gone.

Thank God, he thought. *Thank God, they left for*

the hospital!

He ran down the street and crouched, hiding behind a hedge. When he looked back, he saw Dr. Fritzhauer stumble out of the house and get into the blue Toyota parked in front. Jason knew Fritzhauer was not only smart enough to figure out Roy and Melanie were rushing the baby to the hospital, he was crazy enough to follow them—with the gun.

Jason's mind whirled. What could he do? What! Then he saw it. The parked motorcycle. He jumped on the seat, took a long breath, and remembered. *Three different-colored wires wrapped around each other. Follow the wires to where they end. Release wiring cap. Enter the wires into the sockets . . .*

The motorcycle roared to life. He brought up a program on his phone, then slid the phone into his shirt pocket. He took another breath, pressed down on the gear shift lever, slowly released the clutch, kicked the kickstand down, opened the throttle, and was off—speeding down the slippery-wet streets behind Fritzhauer.

He knew where the hospital was—they'd passed it as they entered Ithaca. But now he wasn't sure how to get there. He had no choice but to follow Fritzhauer. Skimming atop the slick pavement, Jason kept behind the horrific doctor, leaning his body around corners to the right, leaning hard into the left corners. Fritzhauer either didn't see him following or didn't care. He went faster and faster, so that Roy's car now could be seen far ahead and Fritzhauer was gaining on it. *Faster!*

Weaving in and around like a drunk driver, yet completely in control, Jason spun through the streets of Ithaca until Fritzhauer lost control momentarily in a deep water slick.

In the moments it took Fritzhauer to regain control of his car, Roy's car disappeared and Jason blew right past Fritzhauer. The doctor got back onto the road, now chasing Jason—an animal after prey.

Jason sped up even more. He was going fast, *too* fast. He was going eighty, maybe ninety. He didn't care. He felt no fear, only a passion to stop Fritzhauer. He had no actual destination now—he wouldn't go to the hospital, he didn't even know the way. Instead, he suddenly swerved to the right down a one-way street.

Fritzhauer had already crossed the intersection so was forced to slam into reverse to pursue Jason.

Jason's rush over his cleverness instantly drained away, as he spotted Roy's car in the rain-wet mirror behind the doctor. *No!* The hospital must be close. Jason cut down another street, this time in a whole new direction, charging through yellow lights and using a feint to confuse Fritzhauer, twisting quickly from one lane to another, changing direction every few seconds.

It wasn't enough, though. He couldn't shake Fritzhauer, who zoomed right up behind Jason's motorcycle with a terrible engine screech. Any closer and he'd ram Jason's back tire.

I have to do something. Something! His mind spun frantically, searching . . .

It happened in an eye-blink.

An explosion.

A blinding conflagration of billowing black smoke and flames, horrifying as Hell itself and causing the Toyota, with its mad driver hurtling forward way too fast, to crash into the fiery explosion, producing from both vehicles what looked like one single funeral pyre, reaching skyward, blasting out the stars.

EPILOGUE

October 14, 2044

HE STOOD AT THE GRAVE BESIDE MELANIE. ON THIS late autumn afternoon, a sharp blade of grief tore his heart afresh. He passed his hand over his balding hair and let out a choked sound of sigh and sob.

"You loved him," Melanie said softly.

"We were brothers."

"He admired you," she added.

"I scared him that time."

"You didn't mean to."

"Still, I scared him."

The tall, green-eyed teenager standing beside them said quietly, "But he learned the truth soon after." And later, the boy added, "He sure tried to spin it into a funny story."

Jason looked at Adam. "Yes, he did. But it wasn't

funny. At that moment—sixteen years ago—neither Roy nor Melanie knew the explosion was just holographic." Jason turned to Melanie and gently squeezed her hand, saying softly, "I'll always regret how much I scared you both." She smiled and squeezed his in return.

"No," Jason said, turning back to Adam, "I never laughed at Roy's tale."

Adam stroked his curly brown hair as he nodded in understanding, then he looked back down at the grave and said, "I'm glad we had those good years together," and his heartfelt words sailed over the grave like a song.

Jason put his arm around Adam and the two brothers stood together as if under a spell for several moments, looking down at Roy's grave.

From somewhere, a church bell tolled the hour, and in the deep violet sky of twilight, the first three stars winked. Jason winked back at them, then looking at Adam as if in time's mirror, said, "We'd better go. We don't want to be late for your parents' dinner."

They turned away from the grave. Jason took his wife's hand and the three walked quickly up the cemetery path toward the car, and in thoughtful silence, drove to the Kramers'.

ABOUT THE AUTHOR

MAXINE ROSE SCHUR is an award-winning children's book author and travel essayist. She holds a Master of Liberal Arts Degree from Stanford University and is in love with all the arts. In her former lives she worked in New Zealand as a professional stage and TV actress and as a film editor. These days, in addition to writing, she teaches children's book writing and travel writing.

When she can sneak away, Maxine loves to travel and can often be found daydreaming about the next big adventure. She lives with her husband north of San Francisco.

You can find out more about Maxine and her critically acclaimed books at maxineroseschur.com

OTHER BOOKS

by Maxine Rose Schur

The Word Dancer
The Circlemaker
Sacred Shadows
The Peddler's Gift
The Marvelous Maze
Gullible Gus
Marielle in Paris
Pigs Dancing Jigs
Child of the Sea
Finley Finds His Fortune
A Tale of Bread and Thread
When Zissel Got Rich
There's a Babirusa in My Bathtub!
Day of Delight
When I Left my Village
Weka Won't Learn
The Witch at the Wellington Library